LION'S QUARRY

THE MI6 FILES
BOOK 2

BRENT TOWNS

ROUGH
EDGES
PRESS

"A lion sleeps in the heart of every brave man."

—Turkish Proverb

LION'S QUARRY

CHAPTER ONE

VICTORIA, ZAMBORO—0922 HRS (GMT +2)

"Kasinga's had the entire university faculty lined up and shot."

"Good God! Just like al-Bashir did in the Sudan…"

Richard Todd did not turn around. He remained facing forward, awaiting his turn at the customs portal while listening to the whispered conversation behind him. Two British NGO-types were acclimating to the boots-on-the-ground reality of life in Zamboro. So was everyone else in this line of recent arrivals at General Kasinga International Airport, including Richard Todd. The coup had occurred only a week ago, but workmen were already removing Victoria International Airport signage from the concourse under the watchful eye of heavily armed soldiers. Meanwhile, the whispering continued.

"Will we be safe?"

"The government has given assurances… And there

is armed security at the compound. We should be alright."

It was Todd's turn. He stepped forward to the desk, offering his passport and a smile.

"What is the purpose of your visit to Zamboro?" asked the customs officer, glancing at the passport only briefly before scanning Todd with the same glaring intrusiveness of customs officers everywhere.

"Reggie Daniels, of DynaLectrica!" Todd grinned and held out a business card. "Our president is a personal friend of General Kasinga's! I've been sent by way of a courtesy. I'll be calling on the General's offices tomorrow."

The customs officer looked at but did not accept the business card. "For what purpose will you call on the general?" he asked.

"Vacuum cleaners! You'll need lots of 'em, now that you're in charge of the government. All those big buildings to clean! We're prepared to offer steep volume discounts…"

But it was unnecessary to finish. The customs officer was already stamping and handing Todd's false passport back to him and wishing him a pleasant stay in Zamboro. Then Todd was crossing the concourse, swerving past pairs of patrolling soldiers and out through the sliding glass doors to the arrivals lobby. There were only a handful of people present, one of whom was a short, red-headed man in a Hawaiian shirt. He held a sign that read DANIELS. Todd, still in character, navigated toward him with a smile and an outstretched hand.

"Welcome to Zamboro, Mr. Daniels. Can I take your bag?" The red head gave Todd a wink and brought them outside to where his car, an old Ford sedan, was parked by the curb. He waited until they were inside to introduce himself properly.

"Jerry Maxwell, Canadian Security and Intelligence. Welcome to Zamboro, Mr. Todd. We're always glad to help out our good friends at MI-6."

"Nice to meet you." Todd had worked with agents of the Canadian service before and found them to be top drawer. "How long have you been posted here?"

"Since independence twelve years ago." Maxwell started up the car and pulled out. Theirs was the only vehicle on this stretch of road. "Prime Minister Mboya was very well loved so the coup came as a complete surprise to everyone, including our CIA pals at the American embassy. But I guess General Kasinga is something of a cult figure in the Zamboran military. He made his move while Mboya was away on a diplomatic visit to Zaire, then arrested him upon his return. Now Kasinga's the local kingpin—head of the church, head of the military, President-for-Life. Nobody will be deposing *him* anytime soon."

The road broadened into a highway which crossed several miles of plateau before descending toward the capital. Victoria, named for the reigning monarch of the conquering power, was built around a small cluster of white, colonial-era buildings which made up the core of downtown. Todd recognized the Governor General's house and the stock exchange building from photographs he'd seen during his pre-mission brief. Around them bunched the grey and glass facades of Seventies-era office buildings constructed to house the army of bankers, bureaucrats, agricultural and property developers that had labored to turn Zamboro from a backward, subsistence-farming wasteland into something like a modern nation. In the Seventies, these professional ranks had been filled mostly by British and European expats. By the Nineties, they were being edged out by a new generation of ambitious, college educated Zamborans eager for independence.

"Any news about Mboya?" Todd asked.

"Still being held in Mekere Prison," replied Maxwell, turning onto General Kasinga Boulevard, Victoria's main drag, and steering in the direction of the Hotel Presidential. Without taking his eyes from the road, Maxwell pushed a thick brown manila envelope across the seat toward Todd. "I've had some of our ground team pull together a data tout for you."

"Thanks. I'll study this tonight." Todd slipped the packet into a side pocket of his briefcase. "Any word yet on the envoy?"

"Yeah…" Maxwell's tone softened. He almost sounded doubtful. "He's one of ours. Emile Pascale. Did a stint as Foreign Minister under the last government. He's, ah, a bit temperamental…"

Todd made no reply. Pascale had been personally selected by the Secretary General of the UN as his envoy in negotiations to obtain the release of Prime Minister Mboya. MI-6 had pulled strings to get Todd assigned as Pascale's bodyguard. His nominal duty was to ensure Pascale's safety. But his specific orders from MI-6 were to secure the release of Prime Minister Mboya by any means necessary. He hoped Pascale would prove a help and not a hinderance in this regard.

"We've arranged a rental car for you. A Land Rover." Maxwell pulled up at the hotel entrance. "The keys are at the desk. Along with a house-warming present. We're also available for mission support on an as-needed basis." He handed over a business card. "My cell number is on the back. Call anytime."

"Thanks."

"I'm assuming you don't have any other contacts here in-country…"

"I have one," Todd admitted. "We're meeting up for golf this afternoon."

"You play?"

"No." Todd opened the passenger door and stepped out. "He does, though. My role is as spectator."

"Sounds about as exciting as watching paint dry." Maxwell laughed. "Good luck."

CHAPTER TWO

VICTORIA, ZAMBORO—1304 HRS (GMT +2)

"We'll be playing the back nine." Sir Albert Harrison, former British Foreign Office, former Crown Commissioner and ex-Governor General of the Commonwealth nation that had since become Zamboro led them from the clubhouse to the rack of golf bags outside. "I say, you wouldn't happen to have a pistol handy, would you?"

"Ah, no," said Todd. He had left the anonymous brown package containing the 9mm Browning provided for him by Maxwell in his hotel room. "Is there still skirmishing with pro-Mboya loyalists?"

"Oh, no. Goodness, old chap. That was put down a week ago. No." Sir Albert paused and studied the large blue bag containing his Dunlops. "The gun's for the water hazards. Crocs are getting bloody cheeky these days." He peered around. "You don't play, do you?"

"No," said Todd. "I'm from East London. They don't allow Cockneys on golf courses."

"Well, then you can caddy for me since I lost my usual sherpa." Sir Albert began pulling on his golf glove. "We'll start at hole ten. Over here!"

Todd gritted his teeth and shouldered Sir Albert's bag. He disliked the cavalier way the former colonial official dragooned him into this menial service. But he needed Sir Albert's insider knowledge of life in Zamboro if he was to have any chance of securing Prime Minister Mboya's release. He followed Sir Albert to the tee and watched him place a competent shot with his driver three hundred yards downrange.

"Still with Global?" asked Sir Albert. The transnational counterterrorism group had been Todd's berth for two years before he joined Six.

"No, I've moved along in the world. Vauxhall Road for me these days." Todd knew Sir Albert would pick up the reference to the street upon which MI-6 had its address.

"Hm." The former official handed his driver to Todd without a backward glance and set off down the fairway. "So, London has taken an interest, eh? A bit surprising, following a decade of neglect."

"They're concerned about Kasinga." Todd grimaced as his shoe sank into the soggy turf and effluent water soaked through to his sock. "Mboya was a reliable trade ally and regional partner. Kasinga is…unknown. So, they're being cautious."

"Bloody well should be. Man's a butcher!" Sir Albert studied the lie of his ball. "A five iron for this, I should think…"

"Sorry?"

"It's the metal club with the 5 on it. Don't be dull."

Todd handed across the requested club with a sigh. Word was that Sir Albert had spent the decades since

Thatcher drinking in a high-backed chair at the Commonwealth Club. He hoped the old Etonian had at least a few tidbits of useful information left to share. It wasn't until they were on the green that Sir Albert began offering anything useful.

"You *do* know…about the diamonds." He lined up his putt, smacked the ball, and watched it run. "Don't you?"

"No."

Thunk! The ball dropped into the hole. Sir Albert flung the putter back to Todd and said, "That's four. Mark it on the card, would you? And I'll have my three wood for this next hole."

Todd bent, fetched the ball from the hole, and hurried after Sir Albert to the eleventh tee.

"It was good old Cecil Rhodes of fond memory who first scouted the Zamboro field." Sir Albert paused to study the par three ahead of him. "He abandoned it in favor of his and DeBeers' properties in Botswana. The technology to enable large yields in this locale was beyond Victorian. Not so in our day and age. I say…"

He paused. Two kudu had wandered onto the fairway and begun to graze. Sir Albert picked up a rock and flung it at them with a curse. The kudu turned and gazed boredly at the Englishmen before wandering off into the bush.

"Zamboro is rich in other minerals as well." Sir Albert teed up and addressed his ball with the wood Todd provided. "Chiefly cobalt. Very useful for manufacturing those stupid electric vehicles they keep touting nowadays. But Prime Minister Mboya was growing reluctant to allow exploitation of those resources, believing it to be damaging to the environment. And he's bloody right. You ought to see the open pit mine the Chinese dug before he pulled the plug." Sir Albert smacked the ball and sent it sailing. "Bloody awful thing."

"So certain powerful entities—governments, the energy sector—had a vested interest in seeing Mboya gone?"

"They did." Sir Albert handed back the wood and began stalking his ball in the rough. "They seem to be represented by a man named Hua. Big time investor from Beijing. He speaks for the conglomerate of corporate interests—German, Dutch, Indian—that have appeared in the last few weeks, hats in hand, eager to ingratiate themselves with the new President-for-Life."

"What's your opinion of General Kasinga?"

"Bloody lunatic," grumbled Sir Albert, kicking aside loose bits of branch in search of his Titleist. "Plays the sophisticate—professional military man and all that. But he's just a tribal bully from the north. Hold status as a chief and medicine man, if you can believe it. Uses those credentials to strike fear into his political opponents. In the past week there have been something like 1,500 executions. He's not wasting any time setting himself up."

"Any idea where I can find this man Hua?"

"Drop in on a Victoria Chamber of Commerce meeting. It's like the bloody UN, I shouldn't wonder. Ah! There you are. Give my wedge, would you?"

"Wedge?" Todd examined the clubs, flummoxed.

Sir Albert sighed heavily. "You're not a very good caddy, Dickie." He stared into the distance. "Such a shame about Joseph. Best bag carrier in Victoria! That lion wouldn't have stood a chance if he hadn't been sneaking home drunk from his mistress at 2 AM. Still! He was 78. Had a good run. But he is missed. Most dearly."

CHAPTER THREE

Todd sat in his hotel room, watching news footage of the coup on his laptop. Many of the reports featured historical background on the nation, as Zamboro did not often find itself in the western public eye. A recap of the major events included films from independence: crowds dancing in the streets, Zamboran politicians offering grave remarks in the national assembly, and a younger, slimmer Sir Albert ringing down the Union Jack in his Governor General's costume. The mood was hopeful and optimistic, as embodied in the person of the new prime minister.

Julius Mboya had proven to be the right man at the right moment for Zamboran independence. Educated in Britain, he had forsaken a promising career in civil service for life as an agricultural advocate. He had been instrumental in helping the rural poor organize agricultural cooperatives and, where possible, purchase land of their own. This had earned him the respect of many tribal chiefs and had the effect of joining traditional enemies with a common ally. Although he had never sought political office, Mboya had reluctantly run for a seat in the national assembly representing an economically depressed region. His gift for oratory and uniting disparate factions led to a swift rise in his political fortunes.

But all that honeymooning had come to an end when the big electric car producers began rolling in with offers to "develop" areas of the country they deemed "underutilized." The fact that much of that land was used by the poorest Zamborans for subsistence farming caused Mboya to balk. And almost overnight, the man who had been feted as the new face of African progressivism was smeared as backwards in an unforgiving (and click-hungry) western media. Soon afterwards, Kasinga had seen his opportunity and pounced.

Todd checked his watch. It was time for him to meet his protectee at the Canadian embassy.

———

The streets of Victoria were absolutely still and the roads, empty. Not a single pedestrian stirred on the sidewalks and a good many of the store fronts were shuttered. An armed soldier stood on every corner. A state of martial law prevailed in the capital.

The Canadians had beefed up security in light of the coup. A soldier in camo with a C8 and a maple leaf on his shoulder flash checked Todd's ID at the embassy gates and waved him through. Maxwell was waiting for him at the main door.

"How was your trip?" he asked. "Any problems on the road?"

"Not a one." Todd handed over the Browning at the security checkpoint in the lobby. "It's amazing how quiet everything is all of a sudden."

"General Kasinga promised 'law and order.'" Maxwell conducted them upstairs. "Seems he's delivered. He's even managed to win over some of Mboya's allies in the legislature. Of course, parliament has been shuttered since the takeover. Getting that fixed is part of what the UN is hoping to achieve."

"With a little help from His Majesty's Secret Service," muttered Todd.

He followed Maxwell down a lushly carpeted hallway to an elevator with a polished brass door. The ambassador's office was on the top floor—a restricted aerie accessible to a chosen few. The doors parted on a large reception area. A female secretary greeted Maxwell by name then slipped through the wide, tall doors behind her desk to inform the ambassador he had arrived.

"Um, a word about Emile Pascale..." Maxwell hesitated. "He's a top-drawer negotiator. Comes very highly recommended by the Prime Minister's Office. But I feel I should warn you, Mr. Todd, that he can be a bit—"

The ambassador's office door opened and the ambassador himself emerged, the living embodiment of a double-breasted suit. Todd couldn't decide which was brighter—the gleam in his smile or the one in his silver hair.

"...a bit difficult," Maxwell finished.

"Mister *Todd*!" The ambassador bounded forward and pumped Todd's hand athletically. "May I say what a great honor it is to have a representative of His Majesty's government come visit us at our humble little shop. Is Mr. Maxwell taking good care of you?"

"Excellent care, thank you, Mr. Ambassador."

"That's good! Good. Well." He pivoted back to the office and laid a light hand on Todd's arm. "Mr. Pascale is waiting to meet you. I feel I should, er, *warn* you… He can be a bit…" The ambassador paused, searching for the right words. He settled for, "High strung."

"Ah." Todd scratched his cheek. "I see."

The ambassador ushered them through the high, wide doors and into his office. A young man waiting in one of the guest seats immediately sprang to his feet and approached.

"Mister Minister, as you can see, the government of Canada is taking your safety very seriously. Allow me to introduce Mr. Todd from MI-6. He will be your bodyguard."

Emile Pascale looked like he could have walked out of a fashion show. Clear-skinned, bright of eye, and immaculately coiffed, he was the embodiment of the upper-class urban metrosexual. Todd reckoned the bespoke suit he wore cost more than his entire yearly salary at Six. He stuck out a hand. And waited.

Emile Pascale wrinkled his nose. "How disappointing," he said. "I was hoping my bodyguard would be a woman or a person of color. Mr. Todd, are you gay?"

"Excuse me?" Todd actually laughed.

"Oh, I'm very serious," Emile Pascale said seriously. "It's important to practice progressive principles by giving members of underrepresented populations an opportunity to prove their capabilities. I thought I made that very clear, Mr. Ambassador."

An uncomfortable silence fell.

"Uh, no," Todd said at last. "I'm not gay. But there's a chap who works at the liquor store where I buy my ale that might be. Is that good enough?"

"Hardly," sniffed Pascale. "But I suppose, under the circumstances, you'll have to do. It's a shame you don't represent a marginalized population."

"Well, I *am* a combat veteran," Todd said. "I feel we're rather underrepresented. Except among the homeless."

Emile Pascale seemed on the point of objecting to this when the ambassador stepped in and interrupted.

"Why don't we all sit down and have a chat?" he suggested smoothly.

CHAPTER FOUR

VICTORIA, ZAMBORO—1005 HRS (GMT +2)

The ambassador deliberately took his time, calling on his secretary to provide coffee and fussing over the niceties of seating arrangements in order to give everyone time to calm down. Todd suffered through these white-collar delay tactics with resignation. He preferred the coarse language and tough-and-tumble of barracks life, where differences were settled loudly and quickly. Since then, he had learned how civilians—particularly the upper-classes—liked to avoid conflict.

Or disguise it with social gamesmanship, he thought. Pascale seemed like the type who excelled at that sort of interpersonal infighting.

"Ah, lovely!" The ambassador beamed as his secretary deposited a tray of coffee and biscuits on the coffee table before retreating. He distributed cups and poured. Everyone opted for a serving except Todd and Pascale, who ignored each other with studied indifference until the discussion began in earnest.

"Minister Pascale has been sent at the request of the Secretary-General to negotiate the release of Prime Minister Mboya," said the ambassador. "Our position here confers upon us certain advantages. Canada is one of the few nations that has not withdrawn its diplomatic staff or participated in the US-led round of sanctions imposed on General Kasinga's new government. So we're in a position of relative trust compared to the rest of the global community. General Kasinga has agreed to the meeting."

At this point, Pascale lifted his chin, ready to make a pronouncement while staring down his nose at Todd and Maxwell with chilly disdain.

"I am here to represent the civilized forces for the progressive west," he began. "And to remind General Kasinga of his obligations as regards human rights and reciprocal diplomacy."

"In other words, how to behave and play nice with other nations," said Todd. He met Pascale's glare with a mocking smile. He didn't like Pascale. It was important the UN toady remember that Todd was not just a bodyguard but a representative of British Intelligence, which conferred its own diplomatic agency.

"Er, quite," said the ambassador, sitting forward to squelch any conflict before it could arise. "Minister Pascale is eminently qualified to spearhead these negotiations. Mboya's release will be presented as a concession the general can make to appease the global community and restore good faith."

"But it's an entrée—a wedge, if you will." Pascale spread his hands. "If General Kasinga is going to be the head of government here, then he must adhere to global diplomatic norms. Such as the rights of LGBT persons and acceptance of their place in the cultural life of the nation."

Todd raised his eyebrows. The gesture did not go unnoticed.

"You have an objection, Mr. Todd?" Pascale demanded imperiously.

"You're going to push a right-wing strongman to legislate gay rights in a country that's at the epicenter of an AIDS epidemic?" Todd asked.

"What does AIDS have to do with it?"

"Cultural bias. The widespread perception that gay people are the ones getting and spreading the disease," Todd replied. "Doing something like that could spark a pogrom against gay people in this country…in addition to the other groups Kasinga is persecuting. My God, read the room, man."

Pascale was nodding peremptorily and flipping through the pages of a folder before him, plainly ignoring Todd's words.

"The main focus, of course, is securing the release of Julius Mboya," said the ambassador contritely. "Correct?"

After an uncomfortably long pause, Pascale looked up from his documents and said, "Yes."

"The plan is to bring him to the embassy," said the ambassador. "Canada will be offering diplomatic asylum. We'll airlift him from the compound here to an airfield in Tanzania for the flight to Ottawa. It is the government of Canada's belief that Mboya's presence, even from afar, will act to mitigate the worst of Kasinga's excesses. The very possibility of Mboya's return should keep the general in check."

"Assuming sanctions don't do the trick," said Todd.

"Kasinga is an ultra-nationalist," said the ambassador. "Almost like one of the North Korean dictators. He has delusions of 'radical independence' from the global community. Self-sufficiency. That sort of thing. He's undeterred by the sanctions. At least so far."

"It will be our job to impress upon him the power of a united, inclusive, diverse, and equitable west," announced Pascale.

Good luck with that, thought Todd, but said nothing.

————

At Todd's request, Maxwell drove him out to take a look at the prison where Mboya was being held. They set out as soon as the meeting was finished and made their way through the silent, deserted streets toward Mekere prison.

"The bulk of the prisoners there now are political," Maxwell said. "Kasinga has had the entire second floor cleared. That's where Mboya is being held alone under heavy guard."

A few miles outside of town, they pulled off the highway and stepped onto the shoulder of the road. Maxwell handed Todd a pair of binoculars and Todd glassed the distant building. The prison was a concrete and cinderblock fortress with a high wall and guard towers.

"The place is guarded by a crack unit from Kasinga's State Research Bureau."

"So he's got his secret police guarding the enemies of the state." Todd grumbled as he said it. If negotiations failed and Six needed to resort to alternate measures, Mekere would be a tough nut to crack. Any credible bid would involve the deployment of helicopters and special operations troops.

The SAS could do it, he thought. Team Reaper, as well, but that would require Downing Street to call in some heavy political favors.

"Looks like our best bet lies with Minister Pascale," said Maxwell, accepting the binoculars Todd handed back to him.

"I was afraid you were going to say that," he sighed.

CHAPTER FIVE

VICTORIA, ZAMBORO—0205 HRS (GMT +2)

The phone rang beside his bed, waking him at 2 AM. He groaned and sat up in the dark, grappling for the receiver.

"Todd."

"Mr. Todd, it's Emile Pascale." The ex-Foreign Minister's tone was imperious. "I need you. Get dressed and come to the embassy right away." He hung up.

Todd rose and grabbed up his clothes. *What the hell does Pascale need me for at 2 in the morning?* he wondered. They were due to meet with Kasinga's representatives at Government House in less than seven hours. He put the Land Rover's keys in his pocket, tucked the Browning into his belt and left the room.

The soldier waved him through into the embassy compound where a limousine was waiting. Its rear window rolled down as Todd parked beside it.

"Get in," snapped Emile Pascale.

The moment Todd did, the limousine lurched forward. The driver took them out through the gate and onto the roadway, heading deeper into the city.

"Where are we headed?" Todd asked.

Pascale ignored him.

"Look." Todd was growing annoyed. "If you expect me to protect you, I need to know what we're walking into."

"A meeting. It's a meeting," the ex-minister said dismissively, and buried his nose in a file.

All right, Todd thought. He would do his best with the information available to him. But if Pascale refused to share information and got himself killed, it was on his own head. Todd's respect for the man plummeted to a new low.

In a downtown side street, the limo turned into the courtyard of a two-story office complex. The property was clean and well-lit but had obviously not seen use for some time. The limo parked at the entrance. Todd noted a man in a black suit standing on the walkway out front. From the size and stance of the man, Todd could tell at once he was a member of the heavy brigade.

Looks Chinese, he thought.

The driver held the door for them. Emile Pascale swept in through the building entrance, followed by Todd. Two more Oriental men in black suits waited in the lobby. One spoke into a wrist mike as they passed. Pascale took the stairs to the second floor where a woman in a business suit appeared and conducted them into a lit conference room.

"Mr. Pascale. Thank you so much for agreeing to come." A middle-aged Chinese man, the sole occupant of the room, rose from the table and approached, extending a hand.

"Mr. Hua, hello." Pascale shook briefly and took a seat at the table. Todd sat one seat away from him, keeping both men and the door in clear view.

Hua is the spokesman for the local business community, Todd remembered from his discussion with Harrison on the golf course.

Hua began. "It has come to my attention, Mr. Pascale, that you intend to open negotiations with General Kasinga over the release of Prime Minister Mboya from Mekere Prison. We wish you good fortune in your endeavor."

"Thank you, that is correct. And it's *minister* Pascale, not mister. If you please."

"Excuse me. Of course." Hua inclined his head and smiled slightly. Todd thought he detected a slight mockery in the facial expression. "It is about the matter of sanctions that I wish to speak. Doubtless, that will be mentioned in your discussions. I wanted to make you aware, *Minister* Pascale, of an area of concern for myself and my nation. Shīzi Corporation has invested the equivalent of 2 billion American dollars in resource extraction here in Zamboro. Over 800 million of these dollars represent physical assets —excavating equipment, office furniture, computer terminals and servers. The present sanction environment makes it impossible for Mr. Shīzi to retrieve his assets."

Todd did not allow his surprise to show, although surprised he was. Hu Shīzi was a billionaire with a global profile. He maintained a public image as a great humanitarian. His Shīzi Foundation had funded a string of cancer hospitals across Asia and he was a frequent speaker at UN and NGO-sponsored conferences. That he would spend 2 billion of his own corporation's money on a risky venture in unstable Zamboro seemed very uncharacteristic of him.

"Why is this of concern to me?" Pascale snapped.

"Mr. Shīzi has asked me to convey his polite request that the matter of sanctions be introduced into your discussions with General Kasinga. Obviously, a relaxation of sanctions would benefit not only Mr. Shen personally, but Zamboro's trading partners as a whole. It is a desirable outcome. Any influence you can have in this area would earn you the gratitude not only of Mr. Shīzi but also that of the Chinese government."

"I see." Pascale pursed his lips, fingertips toying with the folder in his hands. "Well, Mr. Hua. I don't appreciate your efforts to influence our negotiations. I consider the request impertinent and disrespectful. Representing, as I do, the UN, I am required to remain impartial. Loyal only to the globalist good. I'm sure you understand."

"Of course." Hua tipped his head again. Todd recognized it as a signature move. "I have been asked, in such a case, to remind you of the proportion of your Canadian national debt currently being held in trust by the Chinese government. Economic austerity is making it difficult for us to maintain the interest-to-debt ratio on the account. We may be forced, by circumstance, to call in significant portions of these loans."

Pascale responded to this by inhaling sharply, turning to Todd and muttering, "Out."

Todd rose and left the room.

———

Pascale remained with Hua for an additional twenty-five minutes before emerging, his facial expression carefully neutral. Todd held open the limo door for him.

Pascale said nothing throughout the return drive to the embassy. And Todd didn't press him for any details.

CHAPTER SIX

VICTORIA, ZAMBORO—0823 HRS (GMT +2)

"And so how go the negotiations?"

"We start in half-an-hour," said Todd, adjusting the fit of the phone to his shoulder and examining his hotel room one last time preparatory to leaving. "I'm to meet Pascale at the hotel where the negotiations are being held. The old Empress."

"And what have you found out about the situation in the capital?" Sir Reginald Bull's curiosity was audible in the question. The connection to London was surprisingly good.

Todd had begun his stint at Six as a member of Action Service—that branch responsible for covert counterintelligence and military ops. His background in the Royal Marines and deployment to Afghanistan made him well suited to the role. But his performance had since seen him promoted to his present mission: reporting to Sir Reginald, senior MI-6 counsel, and the Director on missions of unique danger or delicacy.

"I had our Canadian friend drive me out to Mekere prison. Mboya is being held alone on the second floor, guarded by goons of the State Research Bureau."

"Likely torturing him, I shouldn't wonder," grumbled Bull. "Have you confidence in Pascale?"

"No." Todd sighed angrily. "He's a peacock—a strutting, preening, performative little prima donna. And compromised, to boot. He had a secret meeting with a Chinese businessman named Hua. Hua is a wheel in the local community...and almost certainly a Chinese government functionary of some kind. He threatened to put the screws to Canada's debt position if Pascale didn't play ball."

There was a long pause from Bull, then:

"Good God." He cleared his throat. Todd heard paper rustling in the background. "How about the prison? How do you assess our ability to breach and take Mboya, if it comes to that?"

"An SAS team should be able to do it."

"I'll see about having one staged up on that carrier the Americans have prowling about," Bull promised. "SAS will start working out a plan. You, meanwhile, keep an eye on Pascale and our Chinese friends. Gather all the information you can."

"Will do."

———

The Empress Hotel was a relic of Zamboro's imperial past. Todd, whose Cockney ancestors had crewed ships and built bridges and railroads in service of the Empire, just accepted it as given that the upper classes would create zones of privileged privacy for themselves, even in the most far flung reaches of the British Empire. The Empress was such a place.

A large, faux-Greek temple type entrance with Corinthian columns served as a gateway into the grand reception hall. The likes of Cecil Rhodes and junior members of the British aristocracy had stayed here. Not one but two vast staircases rose from the lobby floor to the balcony one floor above which surrounded the great reception hall on all sides. The handles and balcony rails were of burnished brass that gave the dark-grained woodwork a nautical flourish. Todd imagined that British military and merchant sea captains might have billeted here during their lengthy, Spartan peregrinations around the Empire.

Kasinga's government was maintaining its post-coup posture of military readiness. There were four armed soldiers patrolling the lobby. Dark uniformed policemen stood at every doorway. Todd approached the checkpoint and presented the admittance document prepared for him by Pascale, listed under his cover name. The attending officer read it once, folded it, and handed it back with a nod. He was in.

He did a cursory check of the security infrastructure and found that all windows and exterior exits were adequately covered. Kasinga's men had sealed off this section of the city in a six-block radius. There were snipers on the nearby rooftops and a Bell Huey gunship chugged lazily through the skies above like a large metal dragonfly in the tropical heat. Todd pulled out a handkerchief, wiped his face and neck, and checked his watch. Pascale was due to arrive any minute. With a sigh of relief, he returned inside the air-conditioned lobby.

Pascale's motorcade arrived soon afterwards. As he

watched the limousine pull up under military guard, Todd understood why Maxwell had arranged to meet inside the hotel. Kasinga's security cordon was doing a good job of turning away members of Pascale's entourage. To his credit, the pompous little functionary seemed to take it in stride. He had likely been briefed that Todd awaited him within the defended ramparts of the hotel itself.

By the time Pascale made it across the entrance threshold, he had only Maxwell and a female assistant hovering behind him. He addressed himself to Todd immediately.

"This is insane. Kasinga's completely in control here. We're outnumbered and surrounded. Mr. Todd, you're all that stands between me and possible capture by Kasinga's forces."

"I doubt very much they would do that, mister minister," said Maxwell. "Kasinga's government is already skating on thin ice where the UN is concerned. And they've agreed to allow you to have one person in the meeting with you. That will be Mr. Todd. He'll protect you."

Pascale turned to Todd and, for the first time since meeting him, Todd could detect a trace of fear in the man's eyes.

"I'll be right beside you," Todd said reassuringly. "If I drop my hand on your shoulder, that means I've detected a threat and am moving you. When and if you feel that, just drop whatever you're doing and let me guide you where to go. Understand?"

"Understood."

"The plan, in the event a security situation develops, will be to get you out of the building as quickly as possible. I've scouted out the interior and have several different routes committed to memory that will serve us in the event of an emergency." Todd smiled. "Don't worry. We've got you covered."

Pascale nodded. Drawing in deep breaths, he began readying himself for what lay ahead. Todd knew the ex-foreign minister's job was not an easy one. He was under an extraordinary amount of pressure.

"Okay," said Pascale. "Let's go."

CHAPTER SEVEN

A large conference hall had been set aside for the
negotiations. Todd was surprised to see a section of
seats reserved for the press. Ordinarily, negotiations of
this kind would be kept circumspect, held in a clandestine location such as a government office or military
base. But Kasinga wanted to take advantage of the
international interest generated by the event. *He gets to
play the role of the all-powerful leader dictating terms to the
world,* Todd thought. As yet, no press had been admitted
into the room. But no doubt once they were, the negotiators would begin playing to the gallery.

The seating arrangements were like those of a
legislative committee: Pascale, Todd, and Maxwell were
to sit at a long table at the front of the room. Their
interlocutors would face them across a set of tables
elevated on a riser. Flags festooned the row of flagpoles
occupying the space behind those tables and centered
above the flagpoles hung a huge portrait of General

Kasinga. The stage had been set for puffed-up pronouncements and grandstanding. This was obviously meant to be the new government's coming out party.

Todd arranged his seat such that he could keep an eye on both the events at the front of the room and the nearby press gallery. When the representatives from Kasinga's government arrived, they were admitted via a side door and the few photographs taken were by cameras in the hands of military personnel.

Kasinga wants to take the temperature of the meetings before the press is allowed in, Todd thought. It was an intelligent strategy.

The government negotiators were all military officers led by a Colonel, a slender man in glasses. He took his seat at the center chair of the table facing theirs. Once his staff was seated, he began.

"On behalf of General Kasinga and the revolutionary government of the Republic of Zamboro, we call this meeting to order. I am Colonel Ndoke." He paused and studied Pascale. "We welcome the UN team to Victoria to represent the international community's demands upon Zamboro and the revolutionary government."

"Emile Pascale, Colonel," Pascale replied. "Former Canadian foreign minister and representative of the UN Secretary-General. We are not here, Colonel Ndoke, to issue demands. Far from it. The international community recognizes that an unexpected change in government has occurred. Zamboro is still part of the international community. We wish to initiate relations with your government."

"Is it the intention of the international community to maintain its regime of sanctions against us?" Ndoke demanded angrily. "Is it their intention to continue starving and depriving us of technology and material goods?"

"The Security Council is working with member nations to identify the causes of and justifications for their sanctions, which have occurred unilaterally and without coordination from our end. We are eager to get them lifted." Pascale spread his hands. "Releasing Prime Minister Mboya would be an excellent first step toward resuming normal relations with the outside world."

The meetings hadn't been in session five minutes and already the topic of sanctions was on the table. *That was fast,* thought Todd.

Pascale was well and truly compromised.

Colonel Ndoke was declaiming now, full of talk about colonialist legacies and emerging independence movements in Africa. The usual political faff. Todd took the opportunity to scan the hall.

The public and press galleries were still empty. The entryway was being guarded by a pair of armed militiamen but there were a few onlookers scattered around the hall. Todd saw junior officers, soldiers posted as guards, the odd hotel employee that had paused in their duties to listen. A clutch of slender African civilians in dark sunglasses and Banlon shirts lounged near the fire exit. *Those would be agents from the State Research Bureau,* Todd thought. It made sense Kasinga would have secret police present for these meetings. But...

There.

He had felt there was something out of place in the room. Some*one* certainly. Seated at one end of a row of chairs was a Chinese man in a blazer and tie, calmly videotaping the meeting without the slightest objection from either the soldiers or Kasinga's minders from the SRB. Todd got Maxwell's attention and tipped his head toward the videographer. Maxwell glanced over, frowned and went to kneel by Todd's chair to confer.

"You know him?" Maxwell asked.

"No." Todd studied the man as he spoke. "But I'm guessing he's either a representative of Hua's or the government in Beijing."

"It's worth finding out," said Maxwell. He paused as the Chinese man switched off and began packing up his video equipment.

"I'm on it," said Todd.

———

The Chinese videographer was on the move, headed toward a side door. He exited quietly, closing the door behind him. Todd followed and was reaching for the door handle when one of the men in the Banlon shirts and sunglasses moved forward to block him.

"Restricted area, friend," said the secret policeman, a bright smile gleaming within the dark pool of his face. "No admittance without a security pass."

"I'm with the UN delegation," Todd said, keeping his tone cool.

"Sorry." The SRB man raised his hands as if to shrug, but it was obviously a signal as two others began to approach.

"No worries," said Todd. He made for the main entrance.

Emerging onto the hotel steps, he saw the Chinese videographer emerge from the alleyway beside the hotel. He paused at the sidewalk to light a cigarette before turning and heading toward downtown.

With the complete absence of pedestrian traffic, tailing the man on foot would be impossible. Todd made for the Land Rover. It turned over with a twist of the key and Todd pulled onto the road, keeping a block behind the videographer as he made his way briskly along sidewalks empty save for the occasional soldier guarding an intersection.

He's got somewhere to be, alright, Todd thought. And set off in pursuit.

CHAPTER EIGHT

VICTORIA, ZAMBORO—0926 HRS (GMT +2)

The videographer proved easy to follow in the Land Rover. Todd kept several blocks back and cruised slowly enough to keep his distance but not so slowly as to arouse the suspicion of the soldiers on the sidewalk. At the best of times, urban traffic in African cities moved at a dawdling pace. Now it was basically non-existent.

What surprised Todd was the behavior of his surveillance target. The man moved briskly but without panic. And, when stopped by a soldier, he produced a document which caused him to be waved through without delay.

He's got some kind of a pass, Todd thought. Such documents could only have been produced within the past week, and by functionaries of the new government. The videographer had powerful friends in Kasinga's new government.

The man reached an intersection and made a right turn down a side street. Todd made his own right turn one block before, drove down to the next intersection, and waited. He saw the man cross the empty street a block away then turned to follow him and resume his surveillance.

This area of Victoria had long ago fallen into disrepair. As Todd reached the street the Chinese videographer was walking, he noted wooden traffic barriers blocking the road, an upheaval in the pavement as from a bomb and water pooling from a burst water main. This area of town would have seen fighting during the coup. Todd parked his vehicle a hundred yards up from the intersection, locked it up, and continued surveillance on foot.

Traces of the fighting became increasingly apparent the deeper he voyaged into this part of town. Bullet holes scored the walls where AK rounds had pitted the brick facades of buildings and shards of glass from shattered windows sprayed the street. Todd kept to the edge of the sidewalk, where he could duck into a doorway if his quarry turned and looked back, which he did twice. The second time, as Todd waited, a trio of wild dogs crossed the street, noses to the ground, in search of a meal. He waited until they were gone to resume his journey.

The videographer paused outside a tall, windowless structure. He looked around again, forcing Todd to duck behind a trash bin, before stepping through a doorway and vanishing inside. Todd sprinted to the doorway, keeping on the balls of his feet to minimize sound. He reached the edge of the door and peered around.

The building appeared to be some sort of agricultural warehouse. From where he crouched, Todd could detect a ripe smell. In the days since the coup, some of the produce had spoiled. He could see spills of grain and beans from some of the torn bags on the nearest shelving. The shelving marched into the building until vanishing completely in shadow. Todd could hear the Chinese videographer's footsteps ticking on the concrete within. Once again, keeping to the balls of his feet, he set off in pursuit.

It seemed this building had seen its share of combat like the street outside. Todd saw evidence troops might have sheltered in here during the fighting. He passed a portable military cookstove surrounded by empty MRE packaging and was about to hurry past when something caught his eye. He bent to examine the packaging.

Chinese issue, he thought. He could not read Chinese but could differentiate between Chinese and Japanese characters. And he recognized the insignia of the People's Liberation Army on the discarded packaging. Seeing this ignited a simmering disquiet in the pit of his stomach.

The Chinese videographer had entered a small room inset in a wall of the warehouse. Todd spotted him when he switched on the lights. The man had withdrawn his video camera from its case and was hooking it to his phone with a cable. *Getting ready to upload some video,* he thought. It was his last thought before a footstep sounded behind him.

Todd whirled just in time to miss the knife. It hissed through the air where he had been a moment before. Todd barely had time to see the man who held it before he struck out with a sharp front kick, driving his assailant backwards.

Not African, Todd thought as the man recovered and attacked again. He held the knife like a professional—in his right hand, palm up, the handle tucked between thumb and pinkie, slashing underhanded. Todd knew if he miscalculated, the blade would carve a channel into his skin. So, he bided his time and waited for the man to make a mistake.

He came in, slashing back and forth with a kind of controlled frenzy. Todd held his breath, waited, and moved in as the weapon withdrew in a backslash. He kicked out, heel connecting with the side of the man's leg and dropping him to one knee. The knife clattered into darkness. Todd stepped back, lined up to fire a kick at the man's head…and was shocked at the speed and swiftness with which his attacker rose, pivoted and sprinted away into darkness.

Todd turned and saw the office where the videographer had been was now empty, its lights switched off.

Damn! he thought.

———

He returned to the Empress just as the morning session was winding up. At the break, he pulled Maxwell aside.

"What can you tell me about opposition intelligence in Zamboro?" he asked. "Who's playing in the pond these days?"

"It's been pretty quiet, to be honest," Maxwell confessed. "We keep our eyes open, of course. Had a Russian team through a few months before the coup. But they were here to snatch and return home one of their own diplomats for a trial. They weren't interested in Zamboran politics at all."

"How about the Chinese?" Todd asked, producing

an MRE packet from the agricultural warehouse and handing it to Maxwell for examination.

The Canadian gave a low whistle. "Chinese military issue," he said. "That's interesting as hell."

"It certainly is," said Todd. He would have to dig deeper.

CHAPTER NINE

At the end of the first day's round of negotiations, Todd returned to his digs at the Hotel Presidential where he had arranged to meet Maxwell for a drink. They convened in the hotel bar, which was empty. Todd led them to a corner table where they sat, Todd with his soft drink and Maxwell with a beer.

"Well, if success is measured in how many people you manage to piss off, then I'd say the first day of meetings has gone remarkably well for Pascale." Maxwell puffed out a long-suffering sigh and took a swig of beer. "I swear, I thought Colonel Ndoke was going to climb down from the riser and throttle the guy at one point."

"The Chinese have a gun to his head," said Todd. "If he doesn't make an honest effort to get sanctions removed, they'll crater the Canadian economy. That—and *not* Mboya's release—may be the big takeaway from these negotiations. Meanwhile…we've got the Chinese to deal with."

"I've put out a few feelers with my contacts here," said Maxwell. "Any intelligence operation in-country is going to activate some tripwires. If there's a sizable presence from Chinese intelligence in the region, we'll know soon."

"Good. For the moment, things seem to be moving in the direction of Mboya's release. If we don't get him out one way, we'll try another. Meanwhile if the Chinese are behind what's happened here then we need to understand why."

Maxwell nodded. "That will go a long way toward clarifying their plans in the region. I'll keep on it." He downed the rest of his beer and stood. "I've got a meeting back at the embassy. See you at the hearings tomorrow."

"Right."

As Maxwell exited the room, a hotel porter entered bearing an envelope. He made for Todd's table and proffered the envelope, saying it had been left for Todd at the front desk. The note inside was no less cryptic.

I HAVE INFORMATION OF INTEREST TO HIS MAJESTY'S GOVERNMENT. PLEASE MEET ME TOMORROW AT 10 AM AT THE ZAMOBORACORP FIELD OFFICES. — NICHOLAS NERERE, ESQ.

Interesting, Todd thought. He intended to honor the request but had no intention of walking in there blind. He pulled out his cellphone and made a call.

———

It was a short drive from the Presidential to the Commonwealth Club. Despite the atmosphere of tension still prevailing in the capital, the gentrified enclave of colonial nostalgia exuded an aura of humdrum, workaday calm. Todd parked the Land Rover in the lot and hiked up the wide stone steps to the sheltered portico. The entryway door, a monolith of stained oak, stood wide between the stone curtains of the jamb. A Union Jack hung limply in the tropical heat. An African footman in a tuxedo took his name and vanished through a doorway to return a minute later with a smile.

"Sir Albert will see you in the Club Room, Mr. Todd."

Todd found Sir Albert in a high-backed leather chair in the Club Room, which was essentially a vast library with bookshelves stretching to the ceiling. Once, Todd supposed, the little islands comprised of drinks tables surrounded by such chairs would have been crowded with the gentlemen worthies of colonial Zambora. But now the room was all but deserted, the vast hearth quiet, the armies of butlers bustling hither and yon hauling buckets of champagne and trays of canapés replaced by a tired Filipino waiter in a white jacket. Todd arrived just as one was freshening Sir Albert's Pimm's cup.

"Ah, Dickie! Splendid to see you. Care for a Pimm's?"

"Ah, no. Thanks." He took a seat in the nearest leather chair. "I'll just have a beer, thanks," he said to the waiter.

"So!" Sir Albert toasted him. "To what do I owe the audience?"

Todd withdrew the note and passed it over, waiting

as Sir Albert fumbled out his reading glasses and squinted through them at the page. "Oh my," he said gloomily. "How interesting."

"Interesting in what way? You know this Nerere?"

"Not personally, no." He folded the paper and handed it back. "But he was the Minister of the Interior under Mboya. Resigned for health reasons a week before the coup. Saved himself a date with firing squad, most likely…"

"Do you think he knew Kasinga was about to make his move?"

"Doubt it. Even the CIA had no clue. Of course, that is their customary state…" Sir Albert paused, studying the rim of his drink. "Are you planning to meet him?"

"Yes."

"Exercise caution, young Dickie. No doubt our friend Nerere will be under the watchful eye of Kasinga's State Research Bureau. Grisly lot, they are. More so than the usual type that go into intelligence work — present company excepted, of course."

Todd nodded. It made sense that Kasinga would want an eye kept on surviving members of the previous regime. The SRB had appeared with ruthless speed during the coup.

"For a fledgling intelligence department, they certainly have a reputation," he admitted.

"Perfectly warranted, I assure you," replied Sir Albert. "They demanded that all civil servants kneel and recite a pledge of loyalty to General Kasinga. Those that refused were crucified."

"Dismissed? Careers ruined? Property seized? That kind of thing?"

"No." Sir Albert's eyelids drooped. "I mean crucified. Literally. About a hundred of them. Nailed to crosses out at the garbage dump on the outskirts of town." He took a sip of Pimm's. "They're still out there, you know."

Todd clenched his jaw, fighting back an urge to vomit. Crucifixion remained, as it was in the time of Christ, a fearsome and horrific way to die.

"That's good to know, Sir Albert." Todd rose. "Thank you for your time."

"Not at all, old boy." Sir Albert smiled. "If you're still in town next week, be sure to come by for Regency Day. They put out quite a spread."

CHAPTER TEN

VICTORIA, ZAMBORO—0934 HRS (GMT +2)

Todd greeted Pascale and Maxwell at the Empress when talks resumed the next morning. Pascale waited until they were seated at the table to confront Todd.

"You left yesterday partway through negotiations," he sniffed. "You're supposed to be my bodyguard."

"Maxwell was here," Todd replied.

"But *you're* supposed to be here, too. I'm a very important diplomat and I require protection."

"You had Maxwell, the police, and half the Zamboran army covering your six. Under the circumstances, I'd say you were quite safe."

"Is that your professional opinion, Mr. Todd?" Pascale's tone and expression were glacial.

"As a matter of fact, it is." He stood. "Of course, if you're displeased with my performance, I'm sure MI-6 could provide you with a replacement. It should take them about a week…"

"Alright, alright! Sit down! But don't...don't *bugger off* today like you did yesterday!"

Todd smiled and took a seat. And, ten minutes into the negotiations, did exactly that.

———

According to Sir Albert, Zamboracorp had been established under the Mboya government as a replacement for the London-based Crown corporation that had overseen expropriation of the country's natural resources. As such, it was Zambora's largest employer, its green and black heraldic logo an omnipresent feature of life in the capital, adorning busses and buildings, visible in newspapers and official documents, identified as a sponsor to dozens of clubs and organizations. As such, finding the location of the field offices was a simple matter. Within a few minutes, Todd was guiding the Land Rover through the open gates of the facility.

Zamboracorp's field offices were more shunt-yard than office space. Todd parked beside the three modular trailer units where the white-collar folks worked and gazed around at the acres of heavy machinery parked on the site. Front-end loaders, diggers, tractors, back-hoes, and dump-trucks stretched as far as he could see but not a single employee was in sight. The coup's dampening effects were felt even here in the heart of national industry. He let himself out of the Land Rover and went for a stroll.

He found Nerere standing in the shadow of a dump-truck. The former government official was a slender, vigorous man in his early sixties. Dressed in a lightweight tropical suit and straw hat, he was perusing a newspaper when Todd found him. He looked up, offering a relieved smile that it was his expected guest who had found him and not some goon from the State Research Bureau.

"Thank you for coming, Mr. Todd," he said. "My name is Nicholas Nerere."

"How do you know who I am?" Todd asked. "How did you know I was even here?"

"I still have friends in the diplomatic service," Nerere replied. "Kasinga's purges have not succeeded in removing everybody from positions of responsibility. She informed me that a special 'guest' was arriving from London to assist Mr. Pascale. So, I reached out to you."

"You said you had information of interest to His Majesty's government?"

"I do." Nerere folded the newspaper and tucked it under his arm. "And I appreciate your getting directly to the point. It is dangerous for me to be out like this. My information has to do with this." He waved his hand to encompass the heavy equipment surrounding them. "This was the cause of Kasinga's coup."

"Zamboracorp?"

"Peripherally, yes. But more to the point, resource extraction. The western press is making much of Prime Minister Mboya's hesitation to allow development of farmland for mining. He was being pressured by western corporate interests wishing to harvest elements for electric vehicle batteries. But they were *not* behind the coup."

"What are you saying?"

"The Chinese are very interested in the lifting of sanctions," Nerere said. "But not because Shīzi Corporation wishes to withdraw its equipment. On the contrary. They wish to import *more*."

"The diamonds," Todd said flatly. "They intend to bankroll development of the Zamboran diamond fields."

Nerere nodded. "China intends to establish a joint venture between Victoria and Beijing. It will be their entrée into the international diamond market."

Todd's head began swimming with this new knowledge. The pieces were falling into place.

"Was Mboya's government in contact with Shīzi Corporation?" he asked.

"Mr. Shīzi himself visited the capital last year," Nerere said. "It was an important event, observed symbolically with a safari. So, he could visit his namesake."

"I don't follow."

"Shīzi is not just a surname." Nerere smiled. "It is the Chinese word for lion."

———

Todd rushed back to the Empress and resumed his seat just as Emile Pascale and Kasinga's representatives were finishing up the morning session. The ex-minister fired a sour look Todd's way when he sat. Meanwhile, Colonel Ndoke was concluding his remarks.

"…will present to General Kasinga the proposed compromise. We will urge him to release ex-PM Mboya in exchange for a total lifting of *all* sanctions against Zamboro. Further, we will commit ourselves to continued discussions and negotiations going forward."

Pascale seemed pleased, despite his poker face.

Todd had absolutely no doubt this was exactly as he had wished things would turn out.

"I thank you, Colonel Ndoke," he replied. "The international community looks forward to General Kasinga's decision on the matter."

Everyone rose as the negotiating committee stood and made its way toward the exit. Pascale seemed on the point of scolding Todd about his absence but was intercepted by members of the Zamboran press who pestered him for a statement. Todd took this chance to pull Maxwell aside.

"I met with Nerere," he muttered. "He has agreed to provide me with proof that the coup was financed from abroad by Shīzi Corporation."

Maxwell gave a low whistle. "When do you meet him again?"

"As soon as he contacts me." Todd produced his cellphone and checked his text messages. "I expect to hear back soon."

"The sooner the better," Maxwell said. Todd had to agree with him.

CHAPTER ELEVEN

VICTORIA, ZAMBORO—1828 HRS (GMT +2)

Todd's next call with London benefited from another excellent connection. Sir Reginald paid rapt attention as Todd outlined what he had learned.

"All indications at this point are that the coup was deliberately aided and financed from abroad," Todd said. "Nerere claims that it wasn't Mboya's reluctance to do business with the electric car industry but his refusal to cooperate with Shīzi Corporation that led to Kasinga's move. Shīzi and/or Beijing provided direct financing and support for the revolution. All to get a foot in the door of the international diamond market."

"And a bloody lucrative market it is," grumbled Sir Reginald. "Achieving some clarity on the details would be helpful."

"Nerere claims to have documentation." Todd picked up his cellphone and checked the text messages. "He's got back in touch. We'll meet again this evening. He says he's going to hand over everything he has."

"Excellent. Is he asking for asylum?"

"No, Sir Reginald." Todd shrugged. "As near as I can determine, he's still a loyal Zamboran. Doing this for the public good, I shouldn't wonder. As a constitutionalist and parliamentarian, he doesn't welcome Beijing's influence in Zamboro."

"He damn well shouldn't," said Sir Reginald. "They're all over Africa these days. The communist government has sunk billions of pounds into infrastructure and development projects on the continent, and they've got bloody little to show for it. A few working diamond mines would right the ledger in their favor, I should think."

"Agreed." Todd checked his watch. "I should get going."

"I say, Dickie…isn't there a curfew in place at the moment?"

"There is." Todd paused. "A bright white Land Rover will stand out like a sore thumb. So I'll be blacking up and going on foot."

"Take care and come home to us safely, Dickie," Sir Reginald said gravely. "You're an expensive man to replace."

———

Todd waited until full dark before slipping into a sheer black Lycra bodysuit and black balaclava. He stowed the Browning in the pocket of a dark windbreaker he pulled over his top, waited until the hallway outside his room was empty then slipped through the fire exit doors and took the steps to the basement parking garage. The attendant was on duty in his little metal kiosk by the traffic barrier but it was a simple matter to avoid his notice by keeping to the shadows and climbing out to the street over a waist-high cement partition at the elevated section of the garage.

There were no soldiers on duty. They had been replaced by vehicle patrols. No sooner had Todd reached the end of the street than an armored personnel carrier appeared. Todd ducked behind a dumpster as the APC rumbled down the block, flashing a spotlight back and forth across the building facades. He waited until it passed to emerge and continue his journey to the Zamboracorp shunt yard.

What had taken a few minutes by car required a half-hour on foot. At several points in the journey, Todd was forced to dive behind trashcans or duck into door-ways to avoid the APC and, at one point, a roving black car containing members of the State Research Bureau, Banlon shirts and sunglasses in place despite the dark. After about thirty minutes, the fenced Zamboracorp headquarters appeared and Nerere was in the same spot he had been for their first meeting.

"Any problems getting here?" Todd asked. "Did anyone see you?"

"No." Nererc flashed a smile. "My son-in-law works for the SRB. He is loyal to Kasinga, but more loyal to his family. He brought me here."

Todd hoped Nerere was right about his son-in-law's loyalty. "I've been in touch with London. They're aware of your situation. And they're eager to see what you have to offer."

"I have documentation of the government's dealings with Shīzi and his company. Most date from my term of service under Prime Minister Mboya. But I still have sufficient clearance to gain access to government computer systems. Kasinga seems to have overlooked revoking my passwords."

"Excellent. What do you have?"

"Correspondence. Account ledgers. Contracts. A rather comprehensive picture emerges." Nerere reached into a pocket and produced a data drive. "It's all here. Password encrypted."

"What's the password?"

"It's my daughter's name." He smiled again. "Mary."

"Thanks." Todd took the drive and slipped it into his windbreaker. "We'll upload this to GCHQ tonight. You've done your country—and ours—a great service, Mr. Nerere."

The ex-minister inclined his head graciously in acknowledgement.

"The idea of diplomatic asylum was floated in the call with my service earlier today," said Todd. "I wasn't sure that was something that interests you but perhaps we should discuss it."

Nerere seemed puzzled. "Asylum? To?"

"Great Britain. His Majesty's government would supervise your resettlement. Arrange housing, a new identity, employment. You and your family would be safe and under our protection."

Nerere listened to this offer, nodding his under-standing and studying the ground intently as Todd spoke. Todd couldn't help wondering what was going through his mind.

"That is very generous of His Majesty," he said when Todd was finished. "A generous offer indeed. But I must refuse."

Todd's surprise must have been evident in his facial expression, for Nerere continued.

"Don't misunderstand me. I recognize the opportunity it represents. But my place is here. In Zamboro. This is where my tribe is from, where my family lives. We are connected to the land. It is part of our heritage, our identity. It's who we are. I cannot leave."

"Sure. I understand."

"It would be —"

"Wait."

Todd raised a hand sharply and cocked his head. He heard a noise nearby. Was it a squeaking? Or some kind of animal? He closed his eyes to listen.

Nothing.

He opened them again and was about to speak to Nerere when a blast of light and sound erupted as a nearby section of fence collapsed beneath the weight of a car being driven full speed into the compound.

CHAPTER TWELVE

The vehicle cleared the curb at the edge of the lot and landed hard on its front tires, jouncing its snout and rattling its long frame. It took Todd a moment to recognize...

My God, it's a hearse! The station wagon with the extra-long cab and the heavy, bank-vault door in back for sealing in a coffin full of remains. That was all Todd was able to see before he was grabbing Nerere by the jacket and dragging him back behind the cab of a nearby truck. No sooner had the hearse landed and come to a stop than the doors opened and a small army of SBE heavies emerged with pistols drawn.

"Oh my God," Nerere whispered. "That's my son-in-law. He turned on me, on us—"

Todd grabbed and squeezed his shoulder, simultaneously pushing Nerere into a crouch and urging him to pipe down. What did it matter if one of the goons out there was his son-in-law? All were armed to the teeth and ready to kill.

"Come on," he murmured, and guided Nerere back into the depths of the shunt yard, keeping the truck firmly in the line of sight between them and the SRB men until they could meld into shadow.

To Todd's grateful surprise, they managed it. There was no sudden cry, no onrush of footsteps. He could hear Nerere's son-in-law and his fellow goons relaying updates to one another, speaking in the tribal language of the Niska, Kasinga's tribe and the one from which the SRB drew its ranks.

Todd knew the SRB's reputation for cruelty and depravity. Word had it that their agents were often hopped up on drugs, crystal methamphetamine being a preferred favorite. And in addition to the usual sidearms, each carried a *panga*—a carved machete blade that could be shortened for concealment in a sheath worn high on the belt-line. The need for an agent to hide his *panga* accounted for the popularity of Banlon shirts among the SRB.

"This way." Todd tapped Nerere's shoulder. They moved quietly between rows of excavating equipment, the voices of the SRB men fading in the distance. Not having the Land Rover meant Todd would have to get Nerere to safety on foot—a daunting task given the ex-minister's infirmity and use of a walking stick. He had proven spry enough so far. Todd prayed his fitness would hold.

"Do you have a driver coming to pick you up?" Todd asked, whispering despite their distance from the SRB team.

"My son-in-law was the one who drove me here," he

moaned. "He dropped me off just minutes before you arrived."

So, there's a chance they don't know I'm here, Todd thought. He would have noticed the hearse posted up in surveillance. So likely the son-in-law dropped off Nerere, went to SRB headquarters, and came right back with his team in tow.

That gives us an advantage, Todd thought.

He made for the fence. They were deep enough into the yard to be in the thick of the equipment. The fence line wasn't visible, so Todd was orienting from memory and best guess. They had been moving quickly and randomly enough to lose track. But this disadvantage was outweighed by how quickly they had given the SRB men the slip.

Todd slipped out his cellphone and called Maxwell. The agent answered on the third ring.

"Maxwell, it's Todd," he said without preamble. "We're pinned down in the Zamboracorp headquarters lot with a bevy of State Research Bureau coming after us. I'm going to need assistance."

"I've got the diplomatic car," Maxwell said. "They've moved Emile Pascale in here with us at the Hotel Presidential. I'll meet you by the gate."

"Make it fast," said Todd, and hung up. He turned to Nerere. "Come on," he said. "We've got transport on the way. We just have to circle around to—"

Voices.

Todd crouched, bringing Nerere down with him when he did so. His speed saved them. For no sooner had they ducked down behind a nearby pick-up truck than two SRB men ghosted by on the other side. From the tone of their voices, Todd could tell they had no idea he and Nerere were so close. He counted to one hundred slowly, then rose.

Gone.

"Let's go," he urged Nerere. And they were off again through the maze of equipment and vehicles. They were almost to the gate when the SRB man struck.

He came swiftly and silently out of the shadows, arm raised high, his *panga* glimmering in the moonlight. Todd, who was leading the way, turned the instant before he heard the sound of the blade descend into Nerere's shoulder. The man drew in his breath to scream, but his knees buckled as a spray of blood shot up, coating his jaw and ear.

Todd lunged. The SRB man was having trouble uncoupling his *panga* from the meat of Nerere's shoulder. Todd went in with a rugby tackle, hitting the man dead center with everything he had. The SRB man, who was smaller and lighter, was hurled away to crash against the ground with a liquid crunch. Todd landed on his knees, a foot or so away. He reached for the man...

Who was suddenly on his feet...and charging *away* from Todd. Directly at Nerere.

Todd swore and rose, going after him.

The SRB man untangled his *panga*, swung it, and cut Nerere's jugular vein in a clean swipe. This time Todd got him in a chokehold, broke his neck, killing him.

He dropped the body beside Nerere's and resumed course for the gate.

———

Maxwell was waiting. Todd got in quickly and gripped the dash as Maxwell sped back in the direction of Todd's hotel.

"Good to see you," Maxwell said. "How is Minister Nerere?"

"Dead," said Todd quietly. He remained silent for the remainder of the ride.

CHAPTER THIRTEEN

VICTORIA, ZAMBORO—2113 HRS (GMT +2)

Todd returned to his room, showered, and put in a call to Sir Reginald Bull in London. The MI-6 switchboard routed the call through a series of exchanges until locating the restaurant where the attorney was having dinner. When Sir Reginald answered, his voice sounded against a backdrop of tinkling cutlery and distant conversation.

"Bull here."

"Hello. It's Simon," said Todd, using the code cypher for open lines. "I met with our friend. We had an interesting conversation. But he seems to have come down with something."

"Dreadfully sorry to hear," said Sir Reginald. "Is it serious?"

"Yes. Very serious." This was code phrase indicated that the asset ('friend') had been killed. "He left behind some correspondence related to his next-of-kin. We're sorting through it now. Should have some clarity on it in a few hours."

"Yes, well done," said Sir Reginald. "Do send along a copy to Aunt Ginny, would you?" In keeping with the friend/family code set they were employing, 'Aunt Ginny' was cypher for GCHQ.

"Will do, Mr. Bull."

Todd hung up and produced the thumb drive Nerere had provided. If some of its contents actually did come from government databases, then it represented a treasure trove for British intelligence. Todd set up his laptop and was just calling up the digital encryption software when a knock came on the door. It was Maxwell.

"Here." He hoisted a six pack of beer in one hand. The other held his laptop. "Figured you could use a wobbly-pop after tonight's adventure."

"I could. Thanks." Todd accepted a can of beer, pulled the tab, and drank a healthy swig. He leaned forward and typed in the password Nerere had given him for the data drive. The contents of the drive popped up in a fresh window. Todd gestured at it with his beer can. "That's what Nerere was able to pull from the government database."

"Hmm." Maxwell leaned close and peered at the array of files. "There's a lot in there. Perhaps if we split the load and searched through it?"

"That's what I'm thinking." Todd moved in and copied the drive's contents to his desktop before removing it and handing it to Maxwell. "I'll start at the top and work my way down. Why don't you start at the bottom and…?"

"Meet you in the middle? Sounds good." Maxwell

ported the thumb drive into his computer and got to work.

There was a tremendous amount of information on the drive. Todd clicked through the contents of the first sub-folder. Here were bookkeeping records from various government agencies. Todd ran searches and found evidence of payments received from Shīzi Corporation totaling in the hundreds of thousands of pounds. Todd estimated the equivalent of perhaps five million pounds sterling had been received and banked by various ministries in the government.

"When did those payments start?" Maxwell asked when Todd showed him.

"Just a few weeks before the coup," Todd said.

"So Mboya was still in power." Maxwell pursed his lips. "So, either he knew about it..."

"...or there were people within his government aiding and abetting the coup in advance," Todd finished. "Looks like Shīzi was setting himself up for future developments."

They kept looking. Within an hour, they hit paydirt.

"Look at this, Mr. Todd..."

"Call me Dickie."

"Look at this, Dickie." Maxwell jabbed a finger triumphantly at the screen. "E-mail trails. Between Kasinga's staff and Shīzi Corporation."

"Alright." Todd checked his watch. "Let's see if Emile Pascale is still awake."

———

He was. And very annoyed to receive Maxwell's phone call. After a short, angry response from Pascale, Maxwell hung up and turned to Todd.

"He says he'll see us now," the Canadian agent said. Todd gathered his laptop and followed Maxwell to the elevator.

Pascale met them at the door to his room, clad in an expensive silk nightgown and nursing a highball. Todd could tell immediately the diplomat did not care to have his evening cocktail hour interrupted.

"What in God's name?" He squinted at them accusingly. "*Why* on Earth would you disturb me at this hour?"

"We've come across information that's relevant to your negotiations, Mr. Pascale," said Todd, taking the lead. "We feel you should see this."

"What? *What is it?*" Pascale's voice climbed a notch in tone as Todd set down the laptop and opened it to the screen showing the e-mails from Kasinga's staff to Shīzi. Pascale sat, set down his glass with an annoyed *clunk*, and then hunched forward, shoulders tight with anger as he read the stream. After a minute, he relaxed and sat back, crossing his arms.

"Well, well, well," said Pascale. "Would you take a look at that…"

Maxwell and Todd caught each other's eye and grinned.

"This man, Sakir." Pascale tapped the screen. "He's now Kasinga's Minister of Finance. But at the time this was sent, he was on the general staff. What would a member of Kasinga's general staff be doing communicating with a foreign corporation?"

"That was our concern, too," said Todd.

Pascale sat forward and scrolled down, continuing to read. He paused every now and then to sigh and shake his head before resuming his perusal. At length he stood and resumed his drink.

"Gentlemen, I thank you." He sounded uncharacteristically humble. "You were right to bring this to our attention. Remember that I am here as a UN representative. And Kasinga's government has given us certain guarantees as to its purpose and posture regarding international relations. But this puts the lie to much of what they are claiming."

"Negotiating in bad faith," muttered Maxwell.

"Very much so." Pascale's anger was rising now, visible in his face. "This will have to be broached during our discussions tomorrow. It will be handled delicately, but be broached it most definitely will. Can you gentlemen provide me with a copy of this material?"

"Certainly," said Todd.

"Very well." Pascale finished his highball with a single, hard gulp. "We'll bring this with us to the Empress tomorrow. Then we'll see what's what with the good general."

CHAPTER FOURTEEN

VICTORIA, ZAMBORO—1041 HRS (GMT +2)

Pascale waited until just before the negotiations broke for lunch to bring up the contents of the data drive. As promised, he approached the issue carefully. Seated beside him, Todd could sense the envoy steeling himself for what might prove to be a difficult discussion.

"And so," Colonel Ndoke was saying, "we have obtained agreement from the revolutionary council on your proposal to release the former prime minister in exchange for a loosening of sanctions against our government. We are prepared to sign such an agreement at the earliest convenience."

"I have it here," replied Pascale, lifting a sheet from a file folder beside him. "This is an agreement in principle to place sanctions in abeyance in exchange for the release of Prime Minister Mboya. The agreement would come into effect at the moment of its ratification by your government."

Todd heard a roar of shutter clicks behind him. A

full news gallery of reporters, many stringers for international media outlets, had been admitted for this, the last day of negotiations. Kasinga's government had made sure to do everything possible to exploit a positive photo opportunity.

"I have been empowered by the president to sign on behalf of Zamboro," said Col. Ndoke gravely. "I am prepared to sign at once."

"Excellent!" Pascale flashed a smile, hoisted the page and a pen...then paused. "Now...this agreement is predicated upon an understanding that both sides are negotiating in good faith..."

"Of course, of course," muttered Ndoke impatiently from his spot on the rostrum.

"And that the position taken by the Kasinga government represents the will of that government alone," said Pascale. "That Zamboro undertakes this position without let, hinderance, or interference of a foreign power."

"Yes, of course," Ndoke repeated.

"So, it is your position that General Kasinga's position represents a *strictly* Zamboran preference as regards sanctions and all other guarantees?"

"It is." Ndoke's voice held a tone of finality. He was ready for the negotiations to end and recommendations to be implemented.

I bet Kasinga's cracking the whip on that personally, Todd thought.

"Well, then." Pascale's expression was that of the cat that just ate the canary. "I must inquire about a piece of correspondence that's come to my attention." He put down the agreement and picked up another page. "This is a copy of an e-mail exchange between the general staff and the Chinese trade ministry. It is dated two days after the coup that brought your government to power. I'm placing a copy in your hands now…"

A page came forward to accept the offered transcript and place a copy before Ndoke.

"As you can see, on page two there is a discussion of dependencies and priorities governing the expanded trading agreement between Zamboro and the People's Republic of China. The intention of broadening trade and Chinese investment in the country was an explicitly stated goal of the general staff. Releasing Prime Minister Mboya is floated as a possible point of negotiation in trade talks."

The roar of shutter clicks sounded again and Todd could hear muttering between members of an American news crew that hurriedly resumed filming what they had assumed were completed talks. Pascale's "gotchya" tactic was about to make international headlines.

Ndoke read the pages with care, pausing to flip back to the first page and review the entirety of the exchange. He tapped the pages when he was done, muttered to an officer seated beside him, and then spoke to Pascale's concerns.

"Thank you for bringing this to the committee's attention, Mr. Pascale," he said. "This is new information for us and we would like time to review and consult properly with the relevant parties before responding. As such, we will break for lunch and reconvene at 1:30 PM."

With that, Ndoke stood and he and his staff left the room.

———

They returned to the Hotel Presidential, where Pascale immediately went upstairs to make some phone calls. Todd and Maxwell convened in the dining room for a light lunch. Aside from themselves, there were no other guests. A waiter lounged lazily by the kitchen door and a TV in the corner beamed a news broadcast.

"Well!" Maxwell was smiling as he sat. "I'd say Pascale scored a bull's eye, wouldn't you? Ndoke actually showed something approximating a human emotion."

"I'd have to agree." Todd was nodding slowly. "I admit that I wasn't much of a fan of Pascale's at first. But he came through brilliantly. We'll see what Kasinga's government comes back with."

The waiter snapped out of his reverie and came over. At his recommendation, they ordered the soup of the day. The TV in the corner finished broadcasting a soccer match and switched to the local news.

"Pascale's move might prompt sufficient diplomatic pressure to get them to release Mboya early," Maxwell suggested.

"Could do," Todd agreed. The waiter brought them glasses of sweet ice tea. Todd took an appreciative swig. It was some of the best he'd ever tasted.

"I'd give a lot to be a fly on the wall in Kasinga's office right now," Maxwell chuckled.

"You have to wonder what—"

Todd stopped. Something had changed. He scanned the room. They were still alone. He glanced at the TV. And was shocked to see an image of Pascale's face behind the broadcaster.

"...from the State Research Bureau, information that a foreign agent has entered the country posing as a UN nego-

tiator." The broadcaster paused for effect. *"According to sources, the man calling himself Emile Pascale entered the country with the assistance of western powers with the intent of assassinating our dear president-for-life, General Kasinga."*

Todd and Maxwell were instantly on their feet and moving across the hotel lobby toward the elevators. Police cars were already pulling up outside.

CHAPTER FIFTEEN

VICTORIA, ZAMBORO—1214 HRS (GMT +2)

"What the...?" Pascale, phone in hand, stood in his hotel room doorway in his tie and shirtsleeves. "I'm right in the middle of—"

"We're moving," said Todd. He took the phone from Pascale's hand, hung it up, and grabbed the Canadian diplomat by his left elbow.

"What the hell?" Pascale tried to jerk his arm away and blanched when encountering the strength of Todd's grip.

"No worries, Mr. Pascale," said Maxwell, coming up and grasping the right elbow. "We just have to adjust to circumstances right now."

"You just hung up on the Prime Minister of Canada!" Pascale shrieked. *"Now let go of me!"*

"We're on the move," Todd said. And he and Maxwell dragged Pascale out the door and down the hallway. A gloomy stillness prevailed in the corridor despite the chaos unfolding in the lobby downstairs. It was only a matter of time before Kasinga's goons reached this floor. Todd came to a halt outside a door a dozen yards down from Pascale's, knocked and, when there was no answer, pulled out his wallet.

"Best hurry, Dickie," muttered Maxwell, looking up and down the hall.

"What are you doing?" demanded Pascale, his voice an enraged whisper.

Todd did not reply. Removing a laminated ID card from his wallet, he slipped it into the space between the door and the jamb, maneuvering it down toward the knob. Crashing could be heard from the stairwell: the thumping of a dozen pairs of boots as men charged up from below. A rumbling arose from the elevator shaft. They were coming.

Todd closed his eyes, working by feel to wedge the card between the latch and jamb. Fortunately, the Hotel Presidential's rooms had not yet transitioned from old-style knobs to electronic door locks. *There!* With a click, the latch was pushed aside and the door opened.

"Inside," snapped Maxwell, pushing Pascale across the jamb. Todd waited until they were both inside before joining them, pulling the door closed an instant before the elevator opened and a clutch of police and SRB tumbled onto the floor.

"Look at this," Maxwell said.

The empty room was freshly made-up and unoccupied. As voices rose in the corridor outside, Todd locked the door and went to join Maxwell at the window.

"See there?" Maxwell pointed. "Police cars. And you mentioned a hearse?"

Todd peered down. And there it was, the same long,

black hearse that had crashed through the fence into the Zamboracorp yard. Victoria cops and SRB men conferred on the sidewalk beside it, along with another group in dark suits.

"Chinese," breathed Todd. "They looked like state security types."

"I know that one," Maxwell said, pointing. "His name is Shen. A 'trade liaison,' so-called, from the Chinese embassy. But he's an undeclared intelligence agent."

"So, they have Chinese state security coordinating with Kasinga's secret police." Todd's lips firmed in a tight frown. "I'd say that puts the nail in the coffin of Beijing's alibis."

"So, what's the play?" asked Maxwell.

"Will someone *please* tell me what's going on?" Pascale, white-faced and trembling, stood in the middle of the room panicking.

Todd sighed. "Mr. Pascale, there is a warrant for your arrest that's been issued by the government."

"On what charge?" The diplomat's face clouded in rage. "I'm here under diplomatic immunity!"

"Espionage. Conspiracy to assassinate the president."

"What?"

"Keep your voice down," said Todd. He moved past Pascale to the door. He turned the knob, opened it a few centimeters, and stuck his eye to the opening. Pascale's room was visible across the hall and a few doors down. It was open and being guarded by a policeman while SRB men came and went. From the crashing and smashing audible even at this distance, it was obvious they were tossing the room.

Todd eased shut the door and turned back to Maxwell and Pascale.

"They're going to town on your luggage," he told Pascale. "Apparently, diplomatic immunity isn't recognized in General Kasinga's brave new Zamboro."

"He'll answer for this," Pascale growled. His hands curled into fists and he shook his head back and forth slowly. "He can't just flaunt international law and diplomatic norms whenever he feels like it!"

"He can do whatever he wants in his own country," Todd snapped. "Pascale, you'd best wake up. These men will torture and execute you and put your head on a stake. International law isn't at issue here."

"Then what is?"

"Seeing to it that you survive the night."

"So…what do we do know?" Pascale's helplessness seeped into his body language as his shoulders slumped and he lowered his voice despairingly.

"For now?" Todd pulled out a chair and sat. "We wait."

———

The heavy police and SRB presence continued in the hallway for several hours. At one point, an SRB man began knocking on doors, consulting a printed list in his hand. *Probably got a list of occupied rooms on this floor,* Todd thought. Todd heard the door knocks and the muttered discussion between the secret policeman and other guests. But he and Maxwell's plan to repel attackers was not needed. The agent never came and knocked on their door.

Eventually, the SRB team gave up and left, leaving a single policeman posted outside of Pascale's room.

Maxwell cracked the door and kept eyes on the cop. Once he was sure the man was alone, he turned to Todd.

"There's a fire door just down the hall," he said. "Leads to the parking garage. If we can get Mr. Pascale down there, we can hot wire a vehicle and get out of town."

"What's your plan with the cop?"

The Canadian spy grinned. "Leave him to me, Dickie."

Maxwell exited the room.

"What's he doing?" Pascale demanded.

Todd shrugged. He wasn't sure either.

After two minutes, there came a knock on the door. Todd opened it.

"Room service," said Maxwell cheerfully. He bent and dragged the unconscious form of the policeman into the room.

"Put him in the bathroom," Todd said. "Handcuff him to the toilet. And take his radio and gun."

Maxwell did as Todd suggested. And a minute later, they were heading down the hallway to the fire door.

CHAPTER SIXTEEN

VICTORIA, ZAMBORO—1744 HRS (GMT +2)

They did what professional bodyguards call a "quick exfil" of their protectee down the fire steps to the Presidential's underground parking garage. A quick peek through the steel fire door confirmed the lower level was deserted but flush with vehicles.

"What's the play, Dickie?"

"We'll stick together," said Todd. "No waiting with Pascale in here while one of us runs out to hot-wire a car. The SRB is likely to be doing sweeps. If they're not here already, they will be soon."

"Those cars out there." Maxwell gestured with his chin. "Older models. No alarms or fancy electronics in most of them. Should be easy."

"My God, you plan to steal a car?" Pascale looked appalled.

"Perhaps you'd prefer to stay here and let Kasinga's goons capture and torture you?" Todd was running out of patience with the man. Negotiations were over and the crisis was underway. *Time for Pascale to understand where he gets off the bus*, Todd thought.

"I'm a diplomat," Pascale was saying. "In exchange for my immunity, I have to scrupulously obey the laws of any country that I—"

"Well, in this case it's obey the law or get killed. Which is it going to be?" Todd snapped. "Because I'm sure not waiting around to be perforated by bullets. If you've got a martyr complex, more power to you, but Maxwell and I are buggering off. Right, Jerry?"

"Right-o, Dickie."

"Okay, then." Todd turned to Pascale and shrugged. "What's it going to be?"

Pascale's face whitened as he absorbed Todd's and Maxwell's replies. It was just dawning on him that the world beyond the air-conditioned comfort of government offices and chartered jets operated according to a very different set of rules. It was obvious stealing a vehicle would never occur to Emile Pascale in ordinary life. Indeed, he was the sort to drag out his cell phone and raise a hue and cry with the Mounties if he saw such mischief. But here, under the gun in Zamboro, he was plainly expected to compromise. It went against his grain.

"Alright," he said at last. "Go ahead and steal a car."

"This way." Todd shoved open the door and urged Pascale through ahead of him. Their steps echoed off the concrete flooring, reverberating from the concrete walls and ceiling. The parking garage was sealed off from the rest of the world like a pharaoh's tomb. Todd gave thanks for its unique acoustics, which would notify them immediately of anyone's approach.

Row after row of parked cars brooded beneath the cold, halogen lights of the garage. Todd passed vehicle after vehicle, watching a parade of makes, models, and years of production flicker past with each stride he took. Abruptly, he skidded to a stop behind a 1969 model Citroën H Van. It looked like the sort of thing Gendarmes might once have used to transport prisoners.

Or sell ice cream out the back of, Todd thought.

"Here," he snapped. "Jerry? Get Pascale inside…"

"That's *Minister* Pascale to you, Mister To—"

"Jerry, get Loud-Mouthed Arsehole here settled in back. Smack him in the mouth if you must."

"Right-o, Dickie."

As Maxwell hustled a defiant, resisting Pascale into the unlocked vehicle, Todd went around and popped the bonnet. The old French car was no more sophisticated than a '57 Chevy and easily hot-wired. Within three minutes, Todd had the Citroën van running hot. He joined Maxwell and Pascale inside.

"What do we do when we reach a roadblock?" Maxwell asked, settling behind the driver's seat and groping for the stick shift.

"I say we blow right through it," Todd told him. "Once we're outside Victoria, I'll put in a call for an extraction. If the Royal Navy doesn't have anyone nearby, the Yanks will. They'll send a chopper. We'll pile onboard with Pascale and get the hell out of here."

"Sounds like a great plan, eh?" Maxwell shot back. "I'm in agreement! Let's make it happen."

And no sooner were they done talking than Maxwell was pulling out of the parking garage and onto the empty streets.

"You know there are patrols, roadblocks, ghost

cars," muttered Maxwell, depressing the clutch and twiddling the knob of the Citroën's drive shaft. They went from third to fourth gear and the Canadian urged the antique truck ahead like a team of steeds on a horse-drawn sleigh.

"*Look!*" breathed Pascale, and Todd had to hand it to him. The sleazy diplomat was the first to see the improvised checkpoint looming in the intersection ahead. "Jesus, *look!* It's —!"

And indeed, it was. At a nod from Todd, Maxwell slalomed into the turning lane, made a left and took off at right angles to the roadway checkpoint. He floored it the moment the front end stabilized and took off down the street at maximum speed. All seemed well for about thirty seconds. Until Todd noted the hearse materialize in the rear-view mirror.

"Our friends are back," he said.

"Police?" asked Maxwell.

"Funeral for one," Todd said tightly.

"Hang on." Maxwell shifted gears then stabbed the accelerator. The Citroën's engine whined and the van surged forward. The hearse, for all its horsepower, simply didn't have the pep of the French van's engine. They leapt along, gazelle-like, soon leaving the much larger vehicle behind.

Maxwell turned a series of corners, plunging down deserted street after deserted street. Soon, the signage indicated the highway and the route out of town was near. Maxwell and Todd grinned at each other.

"We're in the home stretch now, Mr. Pascale," said Maxwell. "Should be out of the city soon."

"Out of the city and headed *where*?" the diplomat demanded.

"Somewhere safe," said Todd. "First step is to get you clear. Then we'll deal with…"

He trailed off as a military checkpoint appeared in the road ahead.

CHAPTER SEVENTEEN

VICTORIA OUTSKIRTS, ZAMBORO—1820 HRS (GMT +2)

The checkpoint consisted of a trio of bored-looking soldiers, a sandbagged perimeter, and a black-and-yellow striped swing bar that could be lifted and lowered via a counterweight. They were still three hundred yards away but Maxwell was already applying the brakes and slowing down. Todd moved to the Citroën's rear doors.

"Keep them occupied, Jerry." Todd unlatched one of the hinged rear doors and gauged their speed by the swiftness of the pavement passing below. "I'll spring an ambush."

"I'll be ready to back you up," Maxwell replied, reaching under his jacket and discreetly unfastening the snap of his shoulder holster.

Once the blur of pavement below had slowed sufficiently, Todd slipped out onto the road. He kept close to the Citroën's rear to block the soldier's view of him.

When the Citroën braked to a full stop, Todd dropped to his belly on the pavement and scanned for feet.

The Zamboran army wore modern combat boots. Todd saw two pairs standing by the swing-bar's counterweight. He guessed the third was somewhere behind the sandbags. As he watched, one pair of boots moved, stepping around the counterweight and approaching the driver-side window of the Citroën. The man moved with the casual, bored gait of a soldier that had been on duty too long. Todd supposed that vehicles appearing at night were not such a big deal to this lot.

"What is the purpose of your travel?" asked the soldier in English.

"We are complying with a permit violation," Maxwell answered. "We did not have the proper paperwork to remain in the capital overnight, so we're returning as ordered by the major who spoke to us."

"Where did he speak to you?"

"Outside the Empress Hotel. He was from Colonel Ndoke's staff."

Todd saw the second pair of boots move. As his partner engaged the driver, the second soldier moved up the passenger side of the Citroën at a slow, leisurely pace. Todd knew he was scanning for weapons, evidence of explosives, or recent encounters with the military. He would also come around behind the van to check the rear doors.

Todd was ready for him.

The soldier circled around the rear of the van, his eyes still on the ground. Todd killed him with a blow to the larynx, which simultaneously crushed his airway and made raising the alarm impossible. Todd caught his limp form before it could hit the ground. The other soldier, meanwhile, continued to chat with Maxwell.

"Let me see your original paperwork," he was saying.

"The major confiscated it and told us to leave the city." Maxwell paused. "He said that if any soldier demanded our paperwork we were to tell him to contact Colonel Ndoke's staff. So that's what I am telling you. I am in no hurry and will wait."

"Okay, okay," the soldier replied. Todd could sense him making a decision on what to do next. Todd chose that lull to step around the corner, Browning raised, and put a bullet through the man's skull. The dry, flat crack of the pistol reverberated in the tropical night, alerting the third pair of boots, which began thumping...*away* from the checkpoint and into the bush.

"Smart man," observed Maxwell from the driver-side window.

"Definitely a survivor," Todd said. Just then a screech rose from the shadows beside the road bar's counterweight. Todd shone his light on it and revealed a radio operator's backpack, its antenna deployed, its frequency set to the comms traffic station of the local armed forces.

"Zulu Base to Zulu Five... Base to Zulu Five..."

"I wonder if our lot are Zulu Five?" asked Maxwell.

But before Todd could answer, someone else chimed in over the radio frequency:

"Zulu Five all clear."

"Zulu Five clear. Base to Zulu Six, Zulu Six..."

Silence.

Maxwell tilted a smirk Todd's way. "You're on, as they say."

Todd sighed, reached over and plucked the radio mike from its sip. Thumbing the button, he said: "Zulu Six, all clear."

An eternity passed before:

"Zulu Six clear. Base to Zulu Seven, Zulu Seven…"

Todd cast aside the mike, dove back into the van and held on for dear life as Maxwell accelerated down the road and into the interior.

ZAMBORO INTERIOR, SHEKELE PROVINCE—1901 HRS (GMT +2)

Todd had never traveled African highways before and was surprised by how the foliage of the surrounding wilderness crowded inward, suggesting a darkness he knew to be a lie, enclosing them beneath its canopy, enfolding within the enchantment that is the Dark Continent.

When was the last time an agent of British intelligence came out this way? he asked himself. He guessed it was most likely during the days of Rudyard Kipling. Zamboro was deepest Africa—the territory left for cartographers, trappers, and explorers. Until the Dutch abandoned it in 1910, after which it was ceded to Britain following a short and inconclusive war with the Belgians. The outcome seemed to please everybody except the French, who had never forgiven either side.

Bloody Africa, Todd thought. Inconclusive swamp of empires!

Once the British had flocked here, reaping fruits, vegetables, and ivory. Later, nickel and coal. Nowadays, it was post-imperial political conquest. Even if not with explicitly democratic republics, the sales representatives of empire were nonetheless pleased to negotiate defense agreements, weapons contracts, and new understandings with emerging republics, no matter how draconian they might be.

The van was miles deep into the jungle when Maxwell broke the spell of silence.

"Bloody fuck," he said quietly.

"What?" asked Todd.

"I seem to recall that business regarding a…was it a hearse? Like an actual hearse? One that pulls coffins and…?"

YES, IT WAS! The thought shrieked in Todd's mind and he glued his face to the rear window of the Citroën's cab. Behind them was the State Research Bureau hearse, manned by its crew of murderous ghouls. And it was gaining on them fast.

CHAPTER EIGHTEEN

SHEKELE PROVINCE, ZAMBORO—1922 HRS (GMT +2)

The first stretch of road outside of town was well-maintained and dotted with billboards proclaiming the advent of President-for-Life Kasinga's beneficent reign. Zamboran flags hung from the highway lamp posts for five miles outside of town. Then the flags stopped, the road became more rutted, and the thick of the jungle pressed in even more intensely.

There were hills and rivers hereabouts. Todd could tell because of the rushing roar and the rise and fall in elevation. But you would never know either was present given the uniform, ever-present, cloying fauna of the Shekele National Game Preserve. Tourism had always been a big part of Zamboro's attraction, but the preserve itself had become a hotbed of inter-tribal warfare and was now poorly maintained at best, the groundskeepers and game wardens having been driven away by tribal militias and groups of wandering bandits. There were, Todd knew, areas of the country that were still in dispute. For all he knew, they might be driving into one of them now.

"Any sign of the hearse?" Maxwell spoke without turning, his attention glued to the wheel and the road ahead.

"We lost them in that last set of curves a mile back," Todd said.

"More hilly curves coming up," Maxwell replied. "If we can pull another mile or so ahead, we can pull in and post up for an ambush."

"Do it," Todd said.

Maxwell floored the accelerator and the Citroën leapt forward with a thundering growl. The small van had been designed for the narrow, treacherous streets of rural France and Italy, so made short work of the comparatively wide African highway. They flew up into the forested hills, gaining altitude by leaps and bounds. Soon they were in an area where logging roads had been cut into the forest to permit access to some of the valuable timber further upland.

"I think this will do nicely," said Todd.

"This looks like a suitable location," said Maxwell. The impromptu road up ahead shot abruptly uphill and curved behind a thick stand of trees.

"Let's do it," said Todd. Maxwell backed onto the cut trail and braked to a halt behind the stand of trees, the nose of the Citroën pointing at the main road.

Todd studied the lay-out. "If we had a third man, we could do a pit maneuver ambush."

Maxwell nodded. "It's too bad. Because this terrain is perfect for it."

"Perfect for what?" demanded Pascale.

"Uh..." Todd exhaled a frustrated sigh. "A pit maneuver ambush. One man drives a vehicle in to block the road while shooters engage from either side. It's virtually fool-proof."

"It depends on having a third operative capable of—"

"I'll do it," he said flatly. "Drive the vehicle out to block the road. That's what you need done, right?" He turned an angry stare Todd's way. "You don't believe I can do it. You're certain I'd screw it up. Well, you might be right. I'm no nerves-of-steel agent type like you or Maxwell. But I'd rather give this a shot than just hand myself over to the State Research Bureau. I know what's in store for me. Torture. A show-trial. To hell with them. Show me what to do."

Todd smirked. "Alright, mate," he said with grudging admiration.

———

Ten minutes later, he and Maxwell were posted up either side of the main road. They were at staggered intervals to avoid crossfire, but sufficiently close to cover both sides and front and back of their pursuer's vehicle, which was even now chugging up the steep hilly roadway in their direction.

I told Pascale there are three ways to do a vehicle intercept: aggressive, semi-aggressive, and passive. The passive intercept—just blocking the road—was Pascale's assignment for this action. Todd had been surprised by the amount of moxie the government flunky had exhibited. He seemed eager to turn and fight. It was a good, albeit surprising, instinct to see exercised in a political functionary. It made Todd feel a glimmer of optimism about official diplomacy.

Perhaps one day they'll get it right and they won't need to call us as often to patch up their mistakes, he thought.

The sound of the SRB hearse grew louder and louder until suddenly it was swerving around a corner below and chugging up the hill toward their ambush.

"Steady," said Todd in a normal tone, knowing they were too far away to be heard. "Wait for my order!"

Maxwell nodded. Pascale had hopefully heard and was determined to do his part.

The massive vehicle chugged up the hill, closer and ever closer, until it was passing Todd's blind. Then Maxwell's blind. And where…?

Where the hell is Pascale?

And then suddenly the Citroën was leaping out from around its stand of trees and conducting an explicitly aggressive vehicle intercept of the hearse, smashing the van's nose into the hearse's long side panel and driving it nose-first into the shoulder, rear wheels spinning in the chaos and dust.

"YOU FUCKERS!" Pascale screeched from the driver's side window of the Citroën, throwing the SRB men the finger. *"FUCKING ASSHOLES!"*

Todd, fairly doubled over in laughter, regained control of himself and rose, his Browning extended, and opened fire on the hearse's driver side. Across the road, Maxwell was drilling the passenger side with rounds from his sidearm. The vehicle's chassis became riddled with bullet holes. When they ceased fire, no sound remained. Except that of Pascale, who was still raving from the driver's seat of the Citroën.

"God damn you! You damn, damn…god damnables!" *Slam!* The driver's side door swung shut behind Pascale as he alighted, a crowbar in his hands. "You…*assholes!*" He swung the crowbar down on the

hearse's hood, denting it with a deafening *THWANG!*
"You *animals*\!" *THWONG!*

He's mental, thought Todd.

"Ah, sir?" Maxwell rushed up. "Sir?"

"You *fuckers*\!" Pascale swung the crowbar down,
denting the hood afresh. "Utter *bastards!*" Swing!
Schwang!

"MISTER MINISTER, PLEASE LISTEN!" Maxwell
grabbed Pascale's arm and held him still. "It's time to
relax. Stop now. Please stop."

CHAPTER NINETEEN

Maxwell got Pascale moved to the shoulder of the road and continued to calm him down as Todd set to work clearing their trail. Fortunately, the ambush had unfolded as—or, better—than expected. Not a single SRB man had managed to alight from the hearse, and the vehicle itself was more or less still serviceable. Todd muscled aside the driver's corpse, put the hearse in gear, and steered it around such that its snout was facing the drop-off into the trees on one side of the road. Then he got behind the wheel of the Land Rover.

"Out of sight, out of mind?" asked Maxwell jokingly.

"Something like that," said Todd.

"Right. Anchors aweigh, mate."

Todd put the Citroen in gear and nudged the accelerator. The four-cylinder engine bit down with a shriek and the long hearse jumped forward a foot, jostling the bodies inside. Todd nudged again and the hearse's front wheels met and bumped over the road's edge. Todd nudged one last time and the long-bodied vehicle rushed forward into thin air before it began to topple, end-over-end, toward the trees below. It landed amongst the jungle foliage with a crash, a plume of dust, and a rattle, followed by silence.

The jungle had swallowed all trace of it whole. Only they remained.

———

They were well beyond the city's outskirts now. The road was ripped, broken, and completely washed out in sections. They were forced to resort to backroads again and again. Another few miles and crude, impromptu road-signs appeared—primitive art on wood panels that had been nailed to posts sunk into the soft loam.

"Skulls," said Todd as one passed, illumined in the headlamps. "Jerry, what's the story here?"

"We're entering Shekele tribal territory," replied Maxwell. "They're the traditional enemies of Kasinga's tribe. The skull and spear motif you see on the signs is a traditional warning: *you are entering our hunting grounds, keep out.*"

"Does Kasinga control this part of the country?"

"Nominally," answered Pascale. He seemed to have calmed down a bit. "His air force has control of the skies. And he has ground troops stationed in most areas. But some patches, like this area, his generals avoid except in large numbers. Small patrols have a tendency to disappear."

"So, we're somewhat in the clear," Todd said.

"Somewhat," Maxwell allowed. "I wouldn't count on these people as allies, necessarily. They suffered pretty badly under the British. And the Russians were here for a while in the early 1990s. They didn't make a very good impression, either. Our best bet is to lay low and try for the border. Patrols are thinner there. We can slip across into Botswana."

It seemed as feasible a plan as any. Todd kept an eye on the dwindling light as Maxwell steered them off of a back road and back onto a paved surface. The drove for a quarter-mile before encountering a second roadblock.

"Ooooh-kay," said Maxwell, slowing the Citroën. "These guys are Shekele. Militia men. Some of Kasinga's most dreaded enemies."

"What's the play?" Todd asked.

"When all else fails?" Maxwell began rolling down the window. "Tell the truth."

They coasted to a stop before the two 1950s-era sedans parked nose to nose, blocking the road. A group of a dozen men loitered around the cars, some armed, some not. They were a motley collection of rural types, some wearing pressed Banlon shirts and trousers, others in nothing but shorts and sandals. One man, wearing a camo blouse and Detroit Tigers baseball cap appeared to be in charge. He wandered over, cradling an AK in his arms. The jewelry he wore clanked, colliding with the open neck of his blouse as he bent down to address Maxwell through the driver's side window.

"Kasinga not boss here," he said. "You friends of Kasinga, you not welcome here."

"My friend here is a wanted man," said Maxwell, gesturing toward Pascale. "On the run from the State Research Bureau."

"Really?" The man in the Detroit Tigers cap grinned. "You a spy, brother?" he asked Pascale.

"I'm a diplomat from Canada," he replied. "Please, for God sake, help us."

"Help? *You?*" The man in the ball cap turned to his followers and laughed. "Brother, we can barely feed our families! You want our help? You came to the wrong neighborhood!"

At this, all the men laughed. Some chatter erupted in their tribal tongue. Their attitude toward Todd, Maxwell, and their protectee seemed more amused than annoyed.

Todd leaned forward and spoke to the lead man through Maxwell's window. "Could be we have help for you," he said, holding up his wrist. "This watch is worth a thousand pounds Sterling. It's yours if you'll let us through."

"A thousand Sterling?" The leader smirked. "You want to pass through?"

"We need to get to the border," Todd said. "We need to get out of the country."

"Okay, okay." The man in the Detroit Tigers cap was nodding now. "If you want to leave, we have no reason to stop you. This road is clear for ten miles. But then you start coming into Death Brigade territory. You understand?"

"He means Kasinga's commandos," Maxwell explained. "They're like a modern-day Einsatzgruppen. Death squads."

"Death squads, yeah." The head man pointed. "They exterminated the village in the river valley beyond the mountains there. Killed everybody. Two large green trucks. You keep your eyes wide for them, okay?"

"We will," Maxwell promised. "And thank you."

"Here." Todd undid his watch and proffered it.

The leader considered the expensive instrument dangling from Todd's fingers by its leather strap for a long moment before raising a hand and shaking his head.

"You hang onto that, brother," he said. "You may need to bribe someone to get across the border. And we have no use for a watch because we know what time it is." He hefted his rifle. "It's time to fight. It's always time to fight. You go ahead now. And God bless you."

CHAPTER TWENTY

SHEKELE PROVINCE, ZAMBORO—2015 HRS (GMT +2)

The pushed onward through the long, slow African dusk. The twilight fell in weird quadrangles of black and orange, blotting out portions of the road with shadows while painting the air above the tree-tops with fire. In the low-lying areas, details on the ground were difficult to discern, but they were plain enough everywhere else. This section of Shekele Province had been devastated by war. Evidence of tanks and artillery fire was visible in the shredded foliage and impact sites. Large craters in the landscape attested to the murderous aerial campaign Kasinga had waged against his rural opponents—tribal militias up against Dassault Mirage fighter-bombers.

And yet they've hung on, Todd thought, and felt more than a little admiration for the militiamen.

Up ahead, pulses of light flickered in the deepening dark. Maxwell switched off the headlights and brought the Citroën to a halt. The three men waited in the semi-dark, heads cocked, breath held until they heard it again: a low, thunderous growl. Points of light flickered and vanished up ahead.

"Artillery," Todd breathed. "They're still fighting for control of this region."

"It makes sense," said Pascale. "We're close to the border now. Kasinga will want to send a message to the international community that he controls the frontier. We've heard reports that there are ruthless campaigns of repression underway in this part of the country."

"How far from the border *are* we?" Todd directed the question at Maxwell.

"Can't say exactly. But less than an hour's drive." He paused and calculated. "Say between twenty and thirty miles as the crow flies. There will be patrols about, I think."

"Agreed." Todd pulled out his cell phone. "I'll go ahead on foot and clear the path. You hang back, keep the lights off, and keep an open line to my number. I'll guide you verbally."

"Sounds good," said Maxwell.

Todd slipped out of the Citroën's side door and onto the soft shoulder of the road. The sounds of battle, albeit distant, were audible from this vantage. The drone of engines from tanks and helicopters were a faint droning buzz punctuated by the muted *crump* of explosions.

He strode ahead, eyes on the dim road beneath his feet. This section of the main road had been spared the worst of the fighting. He moved briskly, putting a mile between himself and the van before pausing to do a comms check.

"Jerry, you there?"

"Right here, Dickie," came the reply.

"Alright. We're clear for a mile. Pull on up."

Todd waited as Maxwell carefully maneuvered the Citroën along the dark road. He was, Todd saw, keeping to the shoulder. It was a smart strategy to both avoid notice and preserve the option of faking "abandoned vehicle" status in the advent of a patrol.

Todd kept walking. Leapfrogging along like this all the way to the border was a tedious prospect, but necessary if they were to get Pascale out of the country in one piece. Todd strode up the road another mile-and-a-half. There was no change in the volume or sharpness of the combat noises, and no sign of a foot patrol. The road remained in good condition so he was fairly confident they were not headed into any danger.

"We're good up here," Todd reported. "Steady as she goes and no change."

He waited by the roadside as the Citroën shifted gears and began growling its way toward him. That's when headlights winked into visibility in the distance ahead. Todd grabbed up his phone.

"Vehicle coming," he said. "About two miles out."

"Roger that," replied Maxwell. "We'll play dead. Turning off the road now."

Todd went to the edge of the shoulder and slid down into a drainage ditch. The headlights, which had started as pinpricks of lights against the jungle dark, were growing steadily larger now. Todd could tell the vehicle was a ten-ton, the bread-and-butter truck of armies all around the world. Whether it was bringing troops back or heading in for a fresh load, Todd could not tell. But it was coming on, its headlights now the size of small coins. Todd hunkered down in the ditch.

An explosion tore the night, a blast of light that shoved him sideways and filled the air with a deafening roar. Todd shot a look back in the direction of the Citroën.

The front left section of the van was in flames. He noted the headlights of the approaching vehicle had paused three-quarters of a mile off. *Probably radioing in for instructions or back-up,* Todd thought. Keeping to the shadows, he made his way back to the van.

He found Pascale squatting in the bush nearby, a trembling wreck of a man. Todd knelt beside him, scanning for injuries.

"You hurt?" he asked.

"I don't think so." Pascale swallowed. "We just pulled off the road and all of a sudden…"

"Land mine," Todd said flatly. "The country around here will be riddled with them. Particularly by the roadsides. Wait here."

He made his way quickly toward the burning Citroën. The smell of gasoline and burning fabric assaulted him. And, underlying it, the nauseating smell that was so close to cooked lamb…

Maxwell's dead, he realized with a shock.

The form behind the wheel, encased in flames and perfectly still, was nothing more than a human torch. There was no point in trying to rescue him, or risk further exposure to the truck up the road. Now was the time to fade into the shadows and count their blessings. He returned to Pascale.

"It's just us now," he said quietly. "Maxwell's finished but he would have wanted us to carry on. And that's exactly what we'll do. But we'll never make it to the border without a vehicle or without help."

"So, what's the plan now?" Pascale asked, upset plain in his voice but Todd admired his efforts to keep it under control.

"We backtrack to the militia roadblock," he said. "See if they'll help us."

Up the road, the headlights had resumed their approach.

"Come on." Todd took Pascale's elbow and drew him into the jungle.

CHAPTER TWENTY-ONE

SHEKELE PROVINCE, ZAMBORO—2055 HRS (GMT +2)

The sounds of the burning Citroën faded behind them as they made their way into the jungle. Todd hurried Pascale along, wanting to make as much progress as possible before full darkness fell. There would be a moon later, but the hour or so after dusk would be treacherous. Its unfamiliar terrain aside, the jungle was crowded with every kind of danger—poisonous plants and animals, the ever-present soldiers and smugglers that operated in this region close to the border.

"We're going to try to make it to the river we crossed a mile or so back," Todd said. "Then we're going to have to wait a bit for the moon to rise. That should give us enough light to travel by…"

Pascale said nothing. The diplomat was shambling along, head hanging and shoulders slumped. Todd had to hand it to him: for a man accustomed to the comforts of the high life, he was adapting well to an untenable situation. Todd felt confident he could get Pascale to safety—provided the man continued to hold it together.

They traveled until it became too dark to continue. Todd called a halt at the base of a huge tree. Impossible to tell what kind it was in the dark, but the dim shape of its outline suggested a huge trunk—the sort of thing a dozen men holding hands could not encircle. The roots, Todd reflected, must be massive.

"We'll wait here," Todd said quietly.

"Why here?" Pascale asked, looking around fearfully.

"We'll have our backs to something," Todd explained. "That way no one can sneak up on us from behind. And our silhouettes won't be visible. We'll just merge into the shadow of this thing like we're invisible."

"Clever," said Pascale, and Todd almost thought he detected a note of appreciation in the man's tone.

They settled against the base of the huge tree. After a few minutes, it was as if they had become part of the jungle itself. Only the soft noise of their breathing gave them away but it was, surprisingly, almost inaudible. The night jungle was alive with sound and movement. Every now and then, the canopy would ruffle as a bird passed on its nightly errands. Distant fauna hushed and rippled as wind and nocturnal animals made their way through the underbrush. And the odd shriek from a monkey or macaque split the night. Todd found himself remembering surveillance training from his time in the Royal Marines.

"Sit bloody still long enough and you'll see things other people miss," Sergeant-Major Taylor, their instructor, had bawled. "Most people go through life deaf, dumb, and blind.

They see nothing and hear even less. The first step to changing that is to learn how to sit still."

And he was sitting still—perfectly so—when he heard the voices.

They were faint, wispy—the auditory equivalent of a spider's web. Only snatches of sound came to his ears, but they were enough to convince him people were headed this way. It occurred to him that they, too, might be trying to keep quiet.

They move in proper jungle stealth, he thought. Jungle warfare is an art form and clearly these people had studied it. They made barely a sound as they pressed through the foliage. The next clear indication Todd had of their presence was the smell of burning tobacco. Someone had lit a cigarette and was coming closer.

"Hey." He nudged Pascale. "We've got company coming."

"What do we do?" Pascale asked.

"I want you to stay here." Todd pushed himself to his knees. "I am going to see who they are. Once I move off, lie down."

"Why?"

"It will make you less visible and a smaller target." Todd drew his Browning. "Right," he said. "I'm off."

Pascale lay down as Todd moved off through the bush toward the source of the sounds and smell. There was a group of them, no doubt about it. It wasn't sound or smell but rather a sense of *presence* that alerted him. It was almost as if he could sense their nearness. *Instinct,* Todd thought. He had learned to trust his instincts over the years. He did so now.

It was instinct that told him to crouch behind the trunk of a fallen tree an instant before the group materialized. Although it was doubtful they would have spotted him, Todd was grateful for the extra cover. He waited as, by slow degrees, the moon rose, bathing the jungle clearing in light.

There were six of them—rough-looking men in camo and bush hats. One might be tempted to assume they were military but for the way they moved. Theirs was not the ordered march of soldiers but the sly, stealthy maneuvering of the jungle professional. These men knew the area, knew the animals, and (from the look of them) the schedule of the government patrols.

Poachers, Todd thought. Regular hunters travelled by day and camped at night. Only poachers moved through this section of the jungle at this hour. Todd imagined they were en route to some area favored by sleeping game. Quick, quiet kills would net them forbidden prizes and their pay for the month.

Todd watched as they passed by, melting into the trees across the clearing. Then he made his way back to Pascale.

"It's okay," he said in a clear voice. "They're gone."

"Were they hunting us?" Pascale asked.

"No. Although they probably would have if they'd known we were here, I'm confident they were after lesser game," Todd said with a smirk. "Come on. It's time to get moving again."

CHAPTER TWENTY-TWO

SHEKELE PROVINCE, ZAMBORO—2138 HRS (GMT +2)

Under the light of the moon, they continued onwards, traveling until even the distant sounds of battle faded. For Todd, it was like being back in the Commandos and yomping through battlefield terrain. He had learned, during his time in service, how to just put his head down and march. One part of his mind focused on situational awareness while another part wandered, remembering, reflecting, and planning. He could do this all night and all the next day if he had to, but he had doubts about Pascale's stamina.

The diplomat was fine for the first five or six miles. But he soon showed signs of fatigue. To Pascale's credit, he never complained—just did his best to keep up. But Todd could hear the labored breathing, the increasing clumsiness of Pascale's progress as fatigue gripped him. Todd intentionally slowed down. And, when the breathing became a labored rasp, called a halt.

"We'll rest here for a few minutes," Todd said.

"I'm okay," gasped Pascale, stumbling up to him. "We can keep going—"

"Uh, no. It's me." Todd smiled. "I'm actually the one that would like a break, if you don't mind."

"Certainly. Of course," said Pascale. And collapsed onto a mound of soft dirt. Todd took a seat beside him and waited until the man had gathered his breath and managed to relax a bit.

"How much longer do you think?"

"Another hour," said Todd. "Maybe two. The roadblock and the militia's village should be relatively easy to find in this light."

They resumed their trek. They made better progress now that Pascale was rested. But after forty minutes or so, Todd began hearing little grunts and moans of frustration from the man. He ignored these for a while until they started coming with real regularity. Then he paused and turned back.

"Everything okay, Mr. Pascale?" he asked.

"I'm…okay. But I just…"

"Just what?"

"I have to go to the bathroom. Really badly." The strain in Pascale's voice was audible.

"So?" Todd gestured to the trees around them. "Just go ahead and water the fauna. I'll wait."

"It's…more involved than that. I have to…" Pascale paused, frustrated. "There's no toilet paper."

Todd laughed. "No worries, mate." He scanned around until finding a broad-leafed plant. He ran his hands over the underside of the leaves. Finding none of the tell-tale nubbles or sharp points that indicated poison or irritants, he broke off a generous handful and gave them to Pascale. "These will work fine. Just go on off into the trees a bit and do your business. I'll wait here."

"Thank you. *Thank* you!" Pascale seized the wad of leaves and crashed away through the foliage to relieve himself. Todd felt a twinge of sympathy for the man. He had once been in a similar position during a long yomp and knew the discomfort a set of straining bowels could cause a man on the march.

He waited, listening to the jungle sounds around him. The birds were beginning to stir. *Dawn must be near,* he thought. They would have to exercise greater caution as the nocturnal hunters would be on the move, returning to their dens after a night of successful — or unsuccessful — hunting. They didn't want to end up as anyone's main course...

Pascale screamed.

Todd rushed toward the scream, pausing when Pascale's voice faded to be replaced by the sounds of laughter. He crept forward, keeping as low to the ground as possible until the voices were close. Then he peeked through a veil of leaves.

A group of soldiers, Kasinga's men, had surrounded the diplomat. Pascale was struggling to stand and fasten his pants. Todd counted. There were...

Damn! Eight of them!

"What are you doing out here, man?" demanded the leader of the group.

"I got...I mean, my vehicle. It broke down." Pascale's voice was shaking. "My driver went to look for help and —"

"Well, you have found help now," replied the soldier and the rest of them laughed.

Todd pondered his options. He could attack, and possibly even inflict damage on the group. But the chances that Pascale would be taken as a hostage to flush him out or, worse, killed were enormous. That they should bump into a patrol this far into the jungle was unexpected. But now that they had, Todd remained holding very few options.

He gritted his teeth, watching in frustration as the soldiers bound Pascale's hands behind him and led him off into the trees.

———

It took him another hour to find the Shekele village. Wands of smoke rising over the jungle canopy alerted him to the location. Todd followed the breakfast fires until stumbling into a clearing. A campfire burned fitfully in a ring of stones outside a simple hut. The man in the camo jacket and Detroit Tigers baseball cap was sitting on a stump, nursing a beer as he gazed into the flames. He looked up when Todd appeared.

"Hey there, brother." The man grinned. "What happened to your van?"

"We ran over a land mine. And my friends were killed and captured."

The Shekele militia man listened and shook his head when Todd was done. "Government bastards," he said quietly. "I am sorry about your friends."

"Thank you." Todd moved close to the fire and took a seat on an empty stump.

"You want a beer?" The man hoisted his can invitingly.

"No, thank you," Todd replied. "But I need to get back to the capital. Very unlikely I'll make it on foot."

"You try hitchhiking and the police will pick you up, man." The militia man drained his can of beer. "But my cousin Mustafa will be driving into town later with a load of bananas. You can go with him."

"On behalf of His Majesty's government, thank you."

The militiaman laughed. "Next time you see His Majesty, tell him hello from our village. He is welcome to come visit. Anytime."

CHAPTER TWENTY-THREE

VICTORIA, ZAMBORO—0858 HRS (GMT +2)

Mustafa turned out to be a dour, silent man. Todd didn't mind. Dour and silent meant no questions during the trip and that was just fine by him. The only time the elderly, unhappy looking man fished the corn cob pipe out of his mouth to speak was right before pulling over a mile from a checkpoint.

"Get out and get in back," he said. "Under the cargo."

Todd did as he was bid, alighting and circling around to the bed of the truck where he climbed up and burrowed beneath a crush of freshly picked bananas. The mass of great yellow fruit pressed down on him, weighting his shoulders and back and exuding a sweaty, tropical odor. He was thrust around a bit in the bed of the truck as Mustafa resumed the journey. When Todd felt the truck beginning to slow, his hand went to the butt of his Browning.

Footsteps crunching through gravel. The voices of a

soldier asking Mustafa about details of his trip, asking to see ID, and then cracking a witticism. To Todd's ear, the soldier seemed more inclined to joke around than take his duties seriously. But his pleasantries elicited only single syllable replies from dour Mustafa. Then the other soldiers began making fun of him, calling him a sour-puss and a rural bumpkin. When their taunts failed to elicit a response, they tired of the game and bid him pass. Mustafa grunted and threw the truck into gear. A mile or so beyond the checkpoint, he pulled over and let Todd extricate himself from the bananas and return to the cab.

"Those guys were kind of rude," Todd observed.

Mustafa just grunted, chewed on the stem of his corncob pipe, and drove into Victoria.

He dropped Todd at the gate to the Canadian Embassy. After identifying himself, Todd was admitted and allowed to enter the main reception area. He gave his name to the official on duty, who relayed it to the ambassador's office. A guard came and immediately escorted him upstairs, where the ambassador was waiting.

"Mr. Todd, are we ever glad to see you." The ambassador, in shirtsleeves, greeted Todd with a brusque handshake and gestured toward the flat screen TV he and two other staffers were watching. The TV was tuned to a local news station. "You had better take a look at this."

Onscreen, the newscaster was reading his copy with deadly earnestness.

"…reporting the arrest this morning of UN envoy, former Canadian minister Emile Pascale. Pascale was found by a government patrol in the border region, attempting to flee the

country. He was taken into custody and delivered into the hands of the SRB. He is currently being held at the State Research Bureau headquarters in Victoria, pending his trial for espionage."

Good God, what a pig's lunch, thought Todd.

"Mr. Todd, allow me to introduce you around. This is Dave Block, my chief-of-staff. And Lester Hamilton, head of embassy security."

"Mr. Todd, a question." Lester Hamilton, a bald man with a goatee, sat forward ponderously, his muscles bulging the sleeves of his dress shirt. "Where is Jerry Maxwell?"

"Dead." Todd swallowed. "He was driving our getaway vehicle when he ran over a landmine. He was killed instantly."

A moment of sober silence followed the disclosure.

"God," the ambassador said in a whisper. His mouth twitched.

"Did you see Pascale get captured?" asked Block, a slender man in a dark suit.

"I did. He—"

"Well then, why didn't you stop it?"

"There were eight of them," Todd snapped. "If I had intervened, there would have been a shoot-out that, at best, would have ended Pascale's life. At worst, they would have added an MI-6 agent to their interrogation roster at SRB headquarters."

"Mr. Todd had to make a judgment call," said the ambassador. He turned to Todd. "I'm sure you did everything you could. Nobody—" he shot a glance at Block, "appreciates that more than the Government of Canada."

"Of course," said Block smoothly. To Todd, he added, "The question now is how we get him back."

"And Mboya out of jail," fumed the ambassador. "We started the week with one political prisoner. Now we have two. Jesus! Ottawa's going to have my head on a platter..."

"We can appeal to the Director-General of the UN," Block said firmly. "We can bring international pressure to bear—"

"Which will take weeks!" snapped the ambassador. "In the meantime, Mboya gets tried and shot and God knows what happens to Pascale." He was trembling with frustration and rage. "We have our backs against the wall. But good. We've played all our cards."

"Not all of them."

All three men turned to stare at Todd. He reached into a pocket and pulled out the data drive containing the data he and Maxwell had been given by Nicholas Nerere.

"We still have this. It contains every piece of data we could dig up regarding transactions between Kasinga's government and the Shīzi Corporation. It's not the sort of thing either Kasinga or Beijing want going public."

"Didn't you already present some of that to Colonel Ndoke during negotiations?" asked Block.

"We did." Todd nodded. "But only a few pages. This is the motherlode."

"Where's the original?"

"We had it on our laptops."

"The State Research Bureau seized all the luggage from your and Pascale's rooms," protested Block.

"Doesn't matter." Todd waved a hand. "Both our

machines contain GCHQ-encrypted programs on button-down mode. If the access code is not entered the moment the laptops fire up, it wipes the drives. No." He smiled. "This is the only copy left. We can offer to hand it over in exchange for Pascale and Prime Minister Mboya."

Block and the ambassador exchanged a look.

"It's worth a try," Block said finally.

"It is." The ambassador marched to his desk and picked up the phone. "I'll request an audience with the general and present the offer. Then the ball will be in his court." He threw Todd a smile. "Nice work, Mr. Todd. We may manage to scrape our way clear of this debacle after all."

CHAPTER TWENTY-FOUR

Todd was in the embassy mess when the call came through.

"Mr. Todd? Lester Hamilton from embassy security here." He paused. "I've just come from a meeting with the ambassador and Mr. Block. It appears that Kasinga's government has agreed to release Mboya and Pascale in exchange for the data drive."

"Thank God." Todd drained his orange juice and gestured for another. As it was being brought, he said, "Have the details of the swap been sorted?"

"They have. And this is the interesting part." Hamilton lowered his voice as if they were speaking face-to-face. "They want it kept on the low-down. We won't be meeting at the prison, or even at a government agency. They want the exchange to occur after hours in a public place."

"That *is* interesting," said Todd. "You'd think with control of the government they'd be eager to show off their ability to utilize the standing infrastructure. Police cells, military bases, government buildings, that kind of thing…"

"Mr. Block suggests it's a public relations ploy. They don't want the world to see this diplomatic sleight-of-hand."

"Either that or Kasinga doesn't have the control over the country that he claims to have." Todd smiled tightly.

"I understand a colleague of yours is coming in to assist with the exchange," Hamilton said. "Do you have any details on that?"

"Some," Todd admitted. This was a new development for him, as well. "I'm due at the embassy motor pool in a few minutes." He checked his watch. "I'll be signing out an embassy vehicle and using it for a run to the airport. Apparently, Six has a second-stringer coming in from Johannesburg to cover me."

"The more the merrier," said Hamilton. "Your colleague will be welcome here. I'll instruct housekeeping to set aside some quarters for him."

"It's a 'her,' actually," said Todd with a sigh. "An agent I don't know. Code-name Longshanks."

"Long…*longshanks?*" Hamilton laughed. "Sorry, Mr. Todd, but that's just about the goddam *dumbest* cover I've ever heard. MI-6 must be running out of code-names."

"That's not all they're running out of," Todd chuckled. "We're coming up on game-time for me. I'd best be running along."

"We'll see you at the briefing this evening."

"Right."

Todd hung up and made for the embassy motor-pool.

———

There were lots of troops on the highway to the airport. Todd was caught behind a convoy of ten-tons bringing soldiers into the interior. Driving the pale blue Government of Canada jeep sporting both the Canadian and UN flags, he found himself flagged down at the checkpoint and asked to produce documentation. He passed over the forged documents that identified him as an embassy driver from Oshawa.

"Purpose of your trip to the airport?" asked the soldier, glancing over the paperwork before handing it back.

"We've hired a new chef," Todd said. "Was at our embassy in South Africa. We're very excited to have her."

"I see." The soldier, plainly bored, shrugged and waved him on.

Todd pulled up at the airport entrance and parked. Heading into the arrivals terminal, he held up the sign the embassy secretary had made for him. The first woman through the sliding glass doors from the customs portal was a plain, dumpy creature hauling a pink suitcase. She made a beeline for Todd.

"Hiya," she said. "I believe you're looking for me."

"Hello." Todd smiled uncertainly. Longshanks didn't fit the mold of your average MI-6 operative. "We're parked out front."

"Got air conditioning?" she asked, fanning herself with her passport. "It's hotter than an aardvark's asshole."

"Never heard that expression before…" Todd led her through the exit doors and placed her pink suitcase in the rear of the jeep. Once they were ensconced inside and heading back into town, she opened up and introduced herself properly.

"Melissa Longshanks, MI-6," she said. "I've been with the Joburg station for about five years. Our brief is to monitor Chinese influence here on the continent." She produced a pack of chewing gum and jammed a few pieces into her cheeks and began masticating. "And boy, have we been busy…"

"Wait. Longshanks is your actual *surname*?"

"*You have a problem with that?*"

"Uh, no!" Todd smiled generously. "It's a fine name. I just thought it was your code-name."

"They're one in the same." She shrugged. "I guess they figured it was so distinctive, they just let me use it as a cypher."

"Very distinctive."

"Hey. There was a *king* named Longshanks!"

"Any relation?"

"Not that I'm aware of."

Todd smiled tightly and kept driving. "So you've been intercepting a lot of activity from Beijing?"

"Monitoring more than intercepting, yes." She opened her purse and began rummaging through its contents. Todd noted a surprising freight of gum packages and lollypops. "Beijing has gone all-out on infrastructure projects in Africa. Courting governments, offering them generous bailouts or free infrastructure development in exchange for leases on ports and military bases. They're intent on leaving a footprint. All part of their global 'belt-and-road' trade initiative."

"I hear it hasn't been going well."

"It hasn't." Melissa Longshanks spat her gum out the window and unwrapped a lollypop.

Todd put in a call to Reginald Bull to notify him of Longshanks' arrival.

"We're going in for a security pre-briefing prior to the exchange," he told Bull. "This Longshanks. Is she…?"

Bull laughed. "Don't let appearances fool you, Dickie. Melissa is simply top-drawer. Arguably Six's best operative on the continent."

"She looks like she's ready for Weight Watchers," Todd grumbled.

"Now, Dickie. We all have our crosses to bear."

Todd smiled. He hoped Melissa Longshanks would not become his.

CHAPTER TWENTY-FIVE

VICTORIA, ZAMBORO—2346 HRS (GMT +2)

As it turned out, he needn't have worried.

"Ho-*kay*," she said, yanking out a chair and slapping her purse down on the embassy conference table beside Todd. It yawned open to reveal a bouquet of candy bars. "Let's get this show on the road!"

"You eat an awful lot of candy," said Todd. "It's probably not good for you."

"Neither is murder." She tugged loose a candy bar and tore open the wrapper. "Eating calms my nerves. Also helps me think."

Todd peered into her purse. *She must think a lot,* he thought.

The conference room door opened and Block entered, followed by Hamilton from embassy security. They joined Todd and Melissa Longshanks at the conference room table. Block checked his watch before starting.

"Almost midnight," he said. "So we have just over

two hours to debrief. Colonel Ndoke has arranged the meet for 2 AM."

"Where?" demanded Melissa.

"A parking garage downtown, near the old colonial quarter," said Hamilton. "The ambassador has authorized the swap. You'll exchange the data drive for Pascale and Prime Minister Mboya."

"What about cover?" Melissa asked. "We're walking into their territory, just the two of us. What do we have for back-up?"

"I've arranged for four members of CSOR to shadow you," said Hamilton.

"CSOR?" Melissa wrinkled her nose.

"Canadian Special Operations Regiment," Todd said. "They're top drawer." He turned to Hamilton. "What's the plan?"

"CSOR will cover you covertly, so you'll travel in separate vehicles." Hamilton produced a map with the route highlighted in red. "The two of you will leave in the embassy jeep. You'll be followed a short time later by an SUV containing the special operations team. You'll make the turn-off to the garage he—"

"So you're dispatching us—alone—through the streets of Victoria with a security detail following 'at a distance.'" Melissa furiously chewed and swallowed her candy bar and seized up another. "What comms? Air cover? Do we have a tactical fallback plan in case we're attacked en route?"

Block and Hamilton exchanged a glance.

"We don't have air cover," Hamilton said flatly. "Kasinga has imposed a no-fly zone over the capital. And anyway, the only helicopter we have is a civilian model. You'll use encrypted cellphones for communication. As for a fallback plan..." He sat back and spread his hands. "We're open to suggestions."

Todd could sense the favor ebbing away from Melissa, but he had to admit she had a point. *Several good points,* he thought. He was suddenly glad she was onboard.

She sighed. "Alright. Let's set that aside for a moment." She turned to Block. "Who do we have covering the Chinese embassy?"

"*Chinese* embassy?" Block's response was a study in pantomime puzzlement.

Melissa sighed. "Okay. Let me unpack it for you." She held up a hand and began enumerating points on her fingers. "Kasinga and his cronies are obviously in cahoots with Beijing. That copies of this material exist are a threat to the Chinese Communist Party. The Chinese are implicated in this exchange. Do you not think they're going to be active participants in the process of recovering the data?"

"We..." Block cleared his throat. "We hadn't anticipated that."

Melissa swallowed her bite of chocolate, sighed, and threw the rest of the candy bar down on the table in front of her. The absurdity of the gesture, as well as Melissa's quick thinking, endeared her to Todd as few things could. He had worked with female operatives before. They tended to be attractive, athletic, and circumspect. But here was a plain, overweight candy bar addict with an operational mind like a laser.

I wonder if she's as big a surprise in action? he thought.

"We, ah..." Hamilton was sorting through papers. "We don't really have the personnel to spare at this time to watch the Chinese embassy." He looked up with an apologetic smile. "Last round of budget cuts, you see."

"Budget cuts! Well." Melissa flung a hand in irritation. "When I'm rotting away in a State Research Bureau cell after having my fingernails torn out, I'll take solace in knowing that your budget is balanced."

Hamilton, plainly uncomfortable, looked down at his file and said nothing.

"Well, whether the Chinese participate or not," Block said, "CSOR will be present to provide any needed back-up. Let's not—" he said, peering directly at Melissa, "lose ourselves in creeping operational elegance."

"Creeping elegance, huh?" Melissa looked down her nose at Block in a way that suggested she had identified the source of the creepiness.

———

"Bloody idiots!" Melissa thundered, slamming her purse down onto the desk of the office the ambassador had set aside for their use. She wheeled on Todd. "Did you know they were this stupid?"

Todd blinked.

"Er, no," he said quietly.

"Sending us in to negotiate a hostage exchange without *air cover*? No *surveillance* on the agent provocateur? A *jeep* and a squad of Canadian soldiers? That's it? That's all?"

"Apparently…"

"Well! It's a good thing they sent me then." She began rummaging through the chaos inside her purse. "We'll handle this. Get it done. And get both Pascale and Mboya out of the country."

As Todd watched, she dumped her purse upside down. With a crash, an improbable mountain of candies, chocolate bars, toiletries, Kleenex, make-up, and other personal items spilled onto the desk. She then righted the purse and removed a false bottom from which she began to extract machine parts.

As Todd watched, Melissa deftly removed and assembled the pieces for a machine pistol. Todd recognized it as a Sig Sauer Copperhead. The smallest machine-gun available, it was only about fourteen inches fully assembled. Its polymer magazine held twenty 9mm rounds and the gas piston workings could lay down a withering hail of fire. With that amount of firepower in hand, they could almost do without the CSOR escort.

"You pack that in a holster?" Todd asked, astonished as she strapped on an elaborate shoulder holster/sling rig.

"I do, good sir." She affected a curtsey. "A real lady is ready for any occasion."

CHAPTER TWENTY-SIX

VICTORIA, ZAMBORO—0140 HRS (GMT +2)

They met with the CSOR commander in the embassy compound before setting out for the meet. Major Telford was young for his rank but had the confident command presence of a much older man. He stood waiting in the open space between Todd's jeep and the embassy SUV that would transport his team.

"Good morning, Mr. Todd, Ms. Longshanks. I'm Adrian Telford with Canadian Special Operations. Mr. Hamilton's briefed me on your mission."

"Major." Todd nodded. "Hopefully, it should just be a walk in the park. In and out and back here with our people in short order."

"I hope so, too," said Telford. "Meantime, we *are* walking into an unpredictable situation. I thought we should review communications protocols."

"Sounds good."

"We'll use cellphones on an open line." Telford produced his. "Once we're dialed in, we'll just keep an open connection from the moment we leave the compound until we return. And let's keep chatter to a minimum. *Clear* will be the code-sign for all is well. *Break* will be the code-sign for a pause or other break in the mission timeline. *Scramble* will be your signal to us to make our move." He paused. "We'll have your position under observation at all times. We will move on our own if there's gunfire or perceive a threat to you and Ms. Longshanks."

"Sounds good," Todd said again.

"Wait a sec," said Melissa. "What if we've given the 'scramble' signal and then suddenly need to abort?"

Telford raised his eyebrows. "Why don't we just use that word?" he suggested.

"Alright. Clear, break, scramble, and abort," said Todd.

"Anything else we can communicate using the standard NATO alphabet and radio protocols," concluded the major.

Melissa gestured to the front gate. "They'll know we're coming," she said. "Any indication of surveillance on our position?"

Telford nodded. "They've got eyes outside the gate. One man on foot, about a quarter-mile from here. He's got a radio."

"So when we leave, he notifies his SRB cronies," said Todd.

"My guess is they'll set a tail on you when you leave," replied Telford. "We'll hang back and tail the tail. Keep you informed."

Melissa nodded. Todd was glad to see her express some measure of confidence in Telford and his team.

———

They set out just before 2 AM. Todd drove. As they approached the gate, Melissa keyed Telford's number into her cellphone and opened the line. She put it on speaker.

"Clear," she said.

A moment later, Telford's voice came back: *"Acknowledged."*

The embassy gates opened and the jeep glided out onto the empty boulevard. As Todd steered in the direction of the colonial quarter, he noted movement in the rear-view mirror. Their SRB shadow had broken cover and was speaking into a cell phone.

"We've been clocked," he said tersely.

"Let the games begin," sighed Melissa. She grabbed a candy bar from her purse, fiddled with it, and then replaced it, unopened.

The shadowed buildings loomed around them like mountains. Since the coup, there had been power blackouts downtown, reducing the seventies-era office buildings to dark monoliths in the tropical night. There was no movement on the sidewalks or in the streets. The moon ghosted through clouds overhead.

"We've got company," Melissa said abruptly. "I have a contact. They're shadowing us at one block distance. Look…" They approached an intersection. "Now!"

Todd glanced out the passenger window to the intersection one block to their right. Slipping through the intersection, lights off, was the long, low, dark shape of an SRB sedan.

"State Research Bureau," Todd said. "A group of them."

"A *black sedan?*" Melissa wrinkled her nose. "Isn't that a little too cinematic? Baddies in a long, black death car?"

"More practical than cinematic." Todd smirked. "They can carry a crew of them in that thing."

Just then, Telford's voice sounded from Melissa's speakerphone:

"Contact confirmed. We're switching course to shadow them."

"Acknowledged," replied Melissa crisply.

They traveled two more blocks before the sedan appeared in the intersection ahead. Rather than attempt to block the road, they merely stopped at the crosswalk to watch Todd and Melissa float past. He could see no sign of the driver or passengers through the darkly tinted windows. As Todd watched, he saw the SUV containing the CSOR team turn onto the street behind the sedan and brake to a halt one block behind.

Telford's voice came over Melissa's open line:

"Standing by."

"Clear," said Melissa crisply into the speaker before turning and glaring out the passenger window at the sedan. "Bunch of bloody knobs…"

The colonial quarter materialized ahead out of the night, the white facades of the older buildings ghostly white in the street-lamps' haze. The parking garage loomed just beyond the old stock exchange building. Todd glanced into the rear view mirror and saw the hearse tailing them. The MI-6 SUV trailed them at a distance.

"Clear," said Melissa again into the cellphone.

"Acknowledged."

The parking garage had multiple aboveground and subterranean tiers. Per the instructions they had been given, Todd steered onto a ramp that descended below street level. The hearse, he noted, did not follow. The CSOR team had already scouted out the location and picked out their posts, so they would be manning them now.

Assuming they didn't get into a scrape with the SRB crew, he thought.

"And there they are," said Melissa, pointing.

The van leveled out on the lowest underground tier of the garage. Todd spotted the group of vehicles clustered as a group near the center of the underground space. Three large dark sedans and an SRB van sat waiting, presumably intent on Todd and Melissa as they approached.

"Oh, God," whispered Melissa.

"What is it?"

She pointed through the windshield at the nearest dark sedan. From the pennants on the automobile's hood flew two small Chinese diplomatic flags.

CHAPTER TWENTY-SEVEN

VICTORIA, ZAMBORO—0202 HRS (GMT +2)

Todd pulled up and parked one hundred yards from the cluster of vehicles. As he switched the ignition off, he heard Melissa suck in a breath.

"Look," she whispered, nodding to the rear-view mirror.

Todd looked. The sedan was coming down the ramp. It reached the lowest tier of the garage and took up a station at the foot of the ramp one hundred yards behind them, cutting off their egress.

"They're in control of the site," said Todd.

"Contact," Melissa said into the cell phone. "Clear."

"Acknowledged." Telford's voice came back crisply, immediately. *"Posted up and watching."*

"Acknowledged," Melissa replied. She turned to Todd. "This is a pig's lunch."

"Agreed." He sighed, switched off the jeep and pocketed the keys. "No choice now, though, is there?"

"Got to see it through," she agreed. "Shall we?"

"Ladies first."

They exited the jeep, shutting the doors behind them. The parking garage lights gloamed dimly in the haze. The air belowground was stiflingly hot. They began walking toward the cluster of vehicles.

"And here we go," Todd muttered, nodding toward a door opening on the vehicle with the Chinese pennants.

A man stepped out of the driver's side and opened the rear door of the Chinese car. A man alighted—an older, silver-haired Chinese in an impeccably tailored linen suit and wraparound sunglasses.

"Oh, my," breathed Melissa.

"Friend of yours?" Todd asked.

"That's Hu Shīzi." She shook her head in disbelief. "That's the big man himself."

The doors were opening on the other vehicles and more men were alighting. About a half-dozen clustered around Shīzi. A few wore suits. Still others wore military uniforms and sidearms. One held a machine gun. The senior most military man was Colonel Ndoke himself, senior negotiator and member of Kasinga's personal staff.

"The gang's all here," sighed Todd.

They came to a halt twenty yards away from Ndoke, Shīzi, and their minders.

"Where's Pascale?" Todd demanded.

"He is safe." Shīzi smiled when he spoke in his soft, melodious voice. "And he will be returned to you shortly."

"Along with Prime Minister Mboya." Melissa's words were a statement, not a question.

Shīzi nodded. "Mboya, as well. But I believe you

have something for Colonel Ndoke." He tilted his head in the officer's direction.

"You have the entirety of the data we located on your and Pascale's computers?" Ndoke demanded. "We were told you have the sole remaining copy in the hands of your intelligence service."

"We do." Todd reached into a pocket and produced the data drive. "It's all on here. This and the computers in your possession are the only copies we have."

Shīzi examined Todd thoughtfully. "And you, of course, are an agent of British intelligence. Don't bother denying it. Beijing has confirmed your identity —Mr. Richard Todd."

Todd smirked. "At your service," he said, inclining his head in a mocking acknowledgement.

Shīzi stood expressionless for a moment before turning and muttering to a Chinese man in a suit that beside him. The man in the suit nodded but made no other reply.

"So!" Shīzi clapped his hands softly. "All that remains now is to arrange the transfer. Colonel Ndoke. If you would be so kind."

Ndoke turned and barked an order to one of the soldiers, who went to the side of the SRB van and knocked. The panel door rolled aside and an armed soldier alighted, followed by Pascale and a small black man in round eyeglasses who Todd recognized as Prime Minister Mboya. Both were handcuffed. Pascale looked none the worse for wear, but Mboya's suit was rumpled and dirty and he had a large scab on his forehead. It was obvious from his movements and facial expressions that he was in pain.

"Mister Prime Minister," said Todd. "Are you alright, sir?"

"I am...well enough. Thank you." Despite his misery, Mboya managed a smile and a brief laugh. "The men of the State Research Bureau have been most hospitable."

Todd had to hand it to the guy. Under the circumstances, he was showing a great deal of class.

"Mr. Pascale?"

"I never thought I would be so glad to see you again, Mr. Todd," said Pascale. "But you're a sight for sore eyes."

"Now the drive." Shīzi's voice was toneless and cold.

Todd extended the drive. The Chinese man in the suit stepped forward, took it from Todd's hand. He produced a tablet, slipped in the drive, and studied the screen. After a minute, he turned to Shīzi and nodded.

"Everything seems to be in order." Shīzi smiled. "Colonel Ndoke?"

Ndoke barked an order and a soldier moved forward with a key to release Mboya and Pascale from their cuffs. Pascale immediately began walking toward Todd and Melissa. Mboya lagged behind, taking a moment to rub his wrists. As he did this, Colonel Ndoke drew his service weapon, stepped forward, and put a bullet through the back of Mboya's head.

The shot continued to echo even after Mboya's body hit the ground.

"Clear."

Melissa spoke the word calmly and clearly, warning off Telford and the CSOR team. It was a wise move. Any move against Ndoke's and Shīzi's party would erupt in a gunfight that would probably kill everybody in the garage. Todd took advantage of the lull to step forward, grasp Pascale by the elbow, and draw him behind Melissa.

"You've just killed a great man," Todd said quietly. "I hope you're pleased with yourself."

Ndoke holstered his pistol and said nothing.

"There is one more item," Shīzi said.

"And what is that?" Todd asked.

"You, Mr. Todd."

The group of soldiers aimed their rifles at them.

"It is the decision of the Central Committee of the Chinese Communist Party that you will return with us to China."

CHAPTER TWENTY-EIGHT

VICTORIA, ZAMBORO—0232 HRS (GMT +2)

"The hell I will."

Currents of rage coursed through him like electricity. Todd managed to contain his anger, modulate his voice, keep his hands from curling into pre-emptive fists. He would fight rather than submit to this. He didn't care if he died. Capture by a hostile foreign power? That it was an evil to be avoided at all costs had been drilled into him repeatedly throughout his military and intelligence training.

"What's the play?" Melissa's voice was tight beside him. Like Todd, she was affecting nonchalance—controlling herself against the likelihood of a shootout. He had to hand it to her. The woman had real moxie.

"We don't believe in Hell," Shīzi replied coolly. "Only the kind we create for ourselves. And you, Mr. Todd, are in the process of doing that for yourself right now."

"Aces! Now take your pop psychology and stick it

up your arse," Todd snarled, his Cockney rising. He crossed his arms. "I'm not going anywhere with you."

Shīzi considered this briefly. He turned and muttered to Ndoke.

Todd glanced down at Mboya's body where it bled out on the concrete floor.

Bloody animals! he thought angrily.

"Mr. Todd, we have observed that a small coterie of Canadian soldiers has accompanied you as security for this meeting. We know the location of where all four have posted up. Every single one is now in the crosshairs of a Zamboran sniper." Shīzi waved a hand. "Should you persist in this failure to cooperate, they will die."

Todd said nothing.

"Furthermore," Shīzi continued, "Mr. Pascale will be returned to SRB custody. Your lady friend beside you will join him. I am told that survival rates in Zamboro's prisons are minimal."

"What do we do?" whispered Melissa.

"Stand fast," said Todd quietly.

"So." Shīzi's mocking smile returned. "What do you say, Mr. Todd?"

He hated to admit it, but Shīzi had him over a barrel. Losing his own life was one thing. But Shīzi had effectively just threatened to kill six people—Pascale, Melissa, and four soldiers from an allied nation. It was complete blackmail—underhanded, bloodthirsty, and intolerable. Todd's duty in this circumstance could not be clearer.

"Alright." He held up a hand. "But I stay right here where I am until I have confirmation that the others are back safely at the embassy."

"No!" Melissa whispered through clenched teeth.

"Yes," Todd said. "You and Pascale get into the jeep and go. Now."

"Todd—"

"*Right* now," he snarled.

Melissa made no further reply. A professional to the core, she grasped Pascale by his elbow and propelled him toward the embassy jeep. Todd's eyes remained locked on Shīzi's as the engine fired up behind him and the vehicle slid away. Minutes of interminable silence passed until his cellphone bleeped with an incoming text. He pulled his phone out.

> **All personnel safe at the embassy.**
> **Take care. —M.**

Todd read the text, deleted it, and returned the phone to his pocket.

"I'm in your hands," he told Shīzi quietly.

———

They searched and emptied his pockets. Took his weapon. Handcuffed him and led him to the SRB van. Once inside, he was shoved onto a bench where he sat guarded by a half-dozen soldiers as the vehicle started up and drove from the parking garage.

"Thanks for the lift," he said.

"Shut your mouth," snapped the lead soldier.

The van sped through the dark streets. They passed the SRB headquarters building and continued onward into downtown. Although his field of vision was limited, Todd could glimpse the windshield from his seat. The van slowed and turned toward a set of gates manned by armed soldiers. Todd noted the Chinese flag on the gate's signage.

So they've brought me to the Chinese embassy, he thought. *They must be in a hurry to get their prize capture out of the country.*

The van pulled inside the embassy compound and parked. When the panel door rolled open, Todd was ordered to stand. He stepped down to the ground and was taken into custody by a group of Chinese security personnel. Dark suits, sunglasses despite the hour, and not a weapon to be seen among them, although Todd was certain guns were stashed beneath their jackets. He offered no resistance as they marched him to the entrance and inside.

He was patted down again and brought to a windowless room where his handcuffs were fastened to a water pipe, and he was left alone. A half-hour passed before the door opened and one of the Chinese men in dark suits entered.

"Mr. Todd." The man nodded. "My name is Li. I am an operative of Chinese State Security. I am here to take you into custody for transport to Beijing."

"Looking forward to it," Todd said. "I've always wanted to visit China."

Li ignored the witticism and continued. "We will board a government jet for a short trip to Nairobi for refueling, after which our journey will be uninterrupted."

"Will there be an in-flight movie?"

"Mr. Todd, you fail to recognize the gravity of your situation. Once we reach Beijing, you will be remanded to our court system."

"But all my parking tickets are paid up!"

"Our justice system is uninterested in your parking tickets."

"Well, that's a relief!"

"No, you will be put on trial for espionage. It is one of the most serious crimes for which a person can be convicted in our penal code."

"What's the penalty?"

"Ten years of hard labor." Li paused. "In especially serious cases, an individual can be sentenced to death."

"Seems a bit drastic…"

"You have interfered with the affairs of the Chinese government!" Gone was the placid façade. Li was in full rant mode now. *"You have endangered the financial and military security of our nation and thus placed the Chinese people in mortal danger! For this crime, you will face justice at the hands of the People's Court!"*

"You don't say."

"I do say, Mr. Todd." Li moved forward and unlocked the cuff that held Todd to the water pipe, then secured it to his free wrist. "Your final journey has begun."

CHAPTER TWENTY-NINE

NAIROBI, KENYA—0720 HRS (GMT +2)

Todd stared out the acrylic window at the tarmac sweltering in the tropical heat. He and his guards were the only passengers aboard the government of China Boeing 737 that had landed to refuel at Jomo Kenyatta International Airport in Nairobi. The aprons and runways were quiet at this hour, guaranteeing the flight prompt attention from airport authorities. They had already received cordial visits from the Customs and Immigration and airport security supervisors, who had assured the guards that refueling would begin soon and that a delivery of fresh meals was available should they choose to accept it. The pilot assented and the two airport employees left. Li came down the aisle past rows of empty seats and paused before Todd.

"You will have the opportunity to eat a warm meal, Mr. Todd. I suggest you break with the British custom of refusing food from your captors and eat now while you can. Once you enter our facility in Beijing, you will not eat for many days."

"Thank you," Todd said. "I'll take the breaded chicken. And a nice glass of red wine. Whatever the airline carries as house wine will do nicely."

"You will have food," Li said flatly. "You will not have alcohol."

"Can't blame a guy for trying," Todd quipped. He turned back and continued staring out the window. Heat waves were starting to rise from the tarmac. A jet sketched the sky in the distance. Two vehicles circled the edge of the airport terminal and began approaching the plane.

There was no way for him to escape. He had been purposely brought to the toilet and back twenty minutes before landing after being told he would not be permitted to leave his seat while the flight was grounded. So he would eat. Rest and conserve his strength for the ordeal to come.

The two vehicles, a fuel truck and a meal delivery van, approached the plane. The fuel vehicle parked below the wing on Todd's side of the aircraft while the delivery van drove under the tail section and disappeared. Shortly after, a Chinese security officer opened one of the rear doors and prepared to receive the meal delivery lift.

Todd's attention was on the seat back in front of him when he heard a soft *pop* followed by a heavy thud. He swung around in time to see a black man in an airline stewards' uniform step onboard, a pistol in his hands. The pistol, fitted with a silencer, was still smoking. At that same moment, a hatch in the floor flew open and a man wearing mechanic's coveralls sprang into the cabin holding a machine-gun. One of the

Chinese security men shrieked and the man with the gun opened fire. Todd hunkered down.

Bullets sprayed through the cabin. He heard the Chinese security men scream as they were being cut to ribbons. Then: voices. There were multiple intruders. He peeked up over the seat. Three men wearing airport mechanics' coveralls and holding machine guns stood in the aisle. Blood spattered the walls and windows between rows 5 and 10. One of the Chinese security officer's legs poked out into the aisle. The bodies of the other two, meanwhile, would be somewhere behind these rows of seats. A stillness hung in the pause after gunfire. Then a noise obtruded from outside.

A mobile ladder was being driven to the airplane's front hatch. At the top of the steps, Copperhead in her hands, stood Melissa Longshanks in full combat gear. The mobile steps bumped against the fuselage. Then Melissa was pulling the handle from its recessed slot, extending and turning it. The hatch exhaled from the side of the plane and drew outward.

The cockpit door burst open and a final security officer in a dark suit plunged onto the foredeck, a slim black pistol in his hands. As he raised it to fire, the Copperhead stuttered to life and he was torn apart by a withering hail of fire, his body jerking and dancing with the final few slugs before hitting the floor. Then Melissa was striding aboard.

The team dressed as mechanics quickly searched and cleared the rest of the plane. Melissa brought the Chinese flight crew out with their hands on their heads and directed them to sit in passenger seats where she handcuffed them to the arm rests.

Outside, a helicopter was landing beside the plane.

"We'd best hurry," Melissa said, leaning in and

uncuffing him. "We didn't tell the Kenyans we were coming."

"Ah." Todd stood and rubbed his wrists. "Well, I do appreciate your dropping in."

"Not at all, good sir." She headed for the forward hatch, Todd following. "No doubt they'll be curious to see what the shooting was all about."

They stepped out onto the mobile steps. A Royal Navy helicopter, a Merlin, was landing on the tarmac. Jeeps were approaching in the distance. He and Melissa and the team scrambled down the steps and sprinted toward the Merlin where the crew chief was sliding open the hatch.

They boarded in quick order and the chopper rose with dizzying speed. Within moments, they had left the ground behind and turned toward the coast.

"The *Prince of Wales* is moored nearby," Melissa said. "Apparently the chatter between MI-6 and Downing Street has been flying thick and fast. Events in Zamboro have changed the lay of the game board. Your mission is to continue, but you're to be re-tasked."

"How so?"

"We'll be briefed onboard," she said. "A jet arrived earlier with a passenger from London. Apparently, someone from Six."

"They're taking it that seriously?"

"Yes." Melissa sighed and stared out the window. "They are apparently taking it that seriously."

"It beats an all-expenses-paid visit to China."

"That it does."

CHAPTER THIRTY

Their passage out of Kenya went smoothly but was not without incident. Shortly after lift-off, a police helicopter appeared and began to shadow them at a distance. The Merlin managed to climb and increase speed until they lost the observer, and continued to the coastline and the Indian Ocean. They were challenged by radio—a military radar station. The pilot ignored the transmission and sped toward their destination.

"They're persistent," noted Melissa, pulling a packet of gum from her jumpsuit pocket and mashing a few pieces into her mouth.

"They're likely not done yet," said Todd. And he was right.

A few miles from the coast, a Kenyan Air Force jet appeared. The pilot did a fly-past before circling around and challenging the Merlin by radio. The pilot listened before switching channels and making a call of his own. The Kenyan jet, meanwhile, continued circling back in on them. Its more powerful engines and greater range necessitated successive passes as opposed to a constant shadowing. He circled closer and closer, his radio signals to the Merlin's pilot becoming more frequent and insistent. The pilot did not seem overly concerned. Within a minute, Todd could see why.

The Royal Navy F-35 strike fighter streaked in from the sea, cutting a path between the chopper and the Kenyan MiG. The Kenyan pilot took one look at what he was up against, peeled off, and sped back to base.

Todd chuckled as the F-35 escorted them back to the carrier.

———

The HMS *Prince of Wales*, the UK's second of its two Queen Elizabeth-class aircraft carriers, materialized out of the cloud mist and waves to appear in the ocean below. Its deck widened and broadened as the Merlin sank toward it, coming in for a landing with a soft bump that rocked the cabin before settling. The air crew rushed forward to lash down the bird and assist the passengers. Todd, Melissa and the six-man combat team of SAS in their mixed livery of air steward and aircraft mechanic disguises debarked and headed for the nearest hatch below decks.

"Mr. Todd, Ms. Longshanks." The young man in pressed whites waited just inside to greet them. "I'm Quinn, Executive Officer of the *Prince of Wales*. On behalf of His Majesty's Navy, welcome aboard."

"Thank you, commander." Todd grinned. "And thanks for the lift."

"Our pleasure." Quinn chuckled. "I daresay the

Kenyans were less appreciative. But you can't please everybody. We've got a hot breakfast waiting for you in the mess. Afterwards, you'll meet with Sir Reginald Bull."

"Bull?" Todd was surprised. Bull was MI-6's chief counsel and de facto second-in-command. He rarely left the office, let alone London. "He's here?"

"At the PM's orders. Or so we're told." Quinn conducted them downstairs to a mess hall that had been cleared and cleaned following the crew's breakfast. Two trays of food and a pot of coffee sat on a table by the kitchen. "Go ahead and fuel up. Someone will be along shortly to collect you."

———

The food was, contrary to popular belief about Navy cuisine, excellent. Todd and Melissa downed heaps of scrambled eggs, bacon, sausage, and buttered toast, washed down by cups of piping hot black coffee. They were just finishing up when Quinn returned.

"All fed?" he asked. "How was breakfast?"

"Our compliments to the chef!" exclaimed Melissa, downing the last of her coffee and producing a lollypop. "That was really good."

"But, er, not enough apparently," he said, motioning at the lollypop and winking at Todd.

"Just call me Kojak," she said with a lopsided grin.

They followed Quinn through the corridors of the ship to a companionway. The stairs brought them up several decks to the tower structure. A carpeted hallway led them past the captain's quarters, guarded by a Marine who saluted as Quinn passed. Several doors down was a room marked CONFERENCE. Quinn knocked twice and entered.

Seated at the table was the imposing bulk of Sir Reginald Bull. Easily the ugliest man Todd had ever seen, Bull was nonetheless a power player. With a brain like a supercomputer and countless connections in both Parliament and the nobility, he was a unique combination of legal mind, administrative, and operational expertise. He was a known quantity at MI-6, approachable despite his demeanor and invaluable to the Director. It was said even the King occasionally consulted him for advice.

"Well, Dickie!" he grumbled with a fierce smile. "I hear you've been causing all sorts of trouble for General Kasinga and his grisly gang of SRB killers. Well done!"

"Cheers." Todd took a seat at the table.

"And you've met the redoubtable Agent Longshanks." Bull nodded to her. "Many thanks for your help, Melissa."

"My pleasure, Sir Reginald. Chocolate?"

"No, thanks." Bull looked down at the files before him and sorted through the stack. "So! Mr. Pascale is safely en route back to New York to debrief the General Secretary. Kasinga is clinging to his story that Pascale was a spy. Julius Mboya's death has been announced. They're claiming he was killed in an automobile crash."

"Predictable," muttered Todd.

"Quite." Bull cleared his throat. "Our good friend Mr. Shīzi has returned to his home base in Hong Kong. He's doubtless pleased to have the material on the data drive." He paused and stared at both of them. "Five Eyes wants it back."

"Well!" Melissa sounded pleased. "With that kind of momentum behind the effort, no doubt we can count on the assistance of our partners. Particularly the US."

"No."

The word fell like an axe in the quiet room.

"No, I think not." Reginald Bull sniffed and peered at the ceiling. "This particular outing comes with certain details that we feel are best handled *en famille*. We will not be involving the Anzacs. And most definitely *not* our friends at Langley."

"Is there a problem with the CIA?" Todd asked.

Reginald Bull drew in a deep breath before answering.

"I'm afraid there is, Dickie," he said. "A big one."

CHAPTER THIRTY-ONE

HMS *PRINCE OF WALES*—0915 HRS (GMT +2)

The problem began, according to Sir Reginald, as most do in the intelligence world: with a random phone intercept.

"CIA once ran their China station out of Hong Kong," he explained. "The arrangement worked quite well. It allowed them access to both the Chinese mainland and their principal intelligence allies in Taiwan. All that changed in 1997."

On the night of 30 June that year, the Prince of Wales, the British Prime Minister, and the Foreign Secretary met with the Chinese President and Premier at the Hong Kong convention center to formalize the scheduled transfer of sovereignty of Hong Kong from the UK to China. At midnight, the city became a "special administrative region" of China—effectively a democratic and capitalist enclave within the gravitational pull of Beijing. This status, per agreement, would last for fifty years before the city would be enfolded within the Chinese system for good.

"Our friends at Langley were forced to adjust," Sir Reginald continued. "Whereas the CIA had been able to operate from HK more or less with impunity, they were now forced to declare the presence of intelligence officers within consular ranks. For all intents and purposes, the station closed down and Washington's spies went home.

"But gradually, over the course of the next decade, CIA would rebuild its presence in the city. By carefully funneling in personnel under the auspices of trade representatives or NGO employees, they re-established a clandestine presence in Hong Kong. Operational security had been unusually strict and this had paid off. By 2012, they had a functioning substation in Hong Kong and were rebuilding a network of informants on the mainland.

"This included some civil servants and low-level bureaucrats within the emerging government." Bull consulted his files. "The new Hong Kong station contained bleeding-edge cyber capability. Agents were routinely intercepting e-mail and web search traffic from their informants. And others. They were able to build a database of information helpful in providing blackmail material. Particularly useful was the ability to harvest data confirming homosexual tendencies among government employees. Although homosexuality is technically 'legal' in China, Beijing frowns upon overt political activism. And proof of homosexual activity among Party members is unofficially considered subversive.

"The resulting harvest of data—and recruitment of high level government informants—proved a windfall.

"A great deal of this success is due to one man," said Bull. "A man named Arnold Jaxom."

"I've heard of him," said Todd. "Some sort of computer genius, isn't he?"

"Very top drawer," Bull agreed. "Got his start as a cyber officer in the HK station. He was the one delivering the motherlode of blackmail material to Langley. He became the head of the program and, as events progressed, effectively co-chief of CIA's China station."

Bull pushed a black and white photograph across the table. The man pictured was a round-faced type with thick-rimmed spectacles and a bow tie. He looked like the sort more at home in a university faculty lounge than a CIA station.

"Per usual, Jaxom had all the clearances required to interoperate with our team at Six. By 2019, he was a known quantity. His cyber infrastructure was part of the Five Eyes data set. Everything was proceeding along nicely."

The problems began the following year. Jaxom took vacation and travelled to Africa. Per CIA procedures, he was required to list and declare the names of all nations and foreign officials with whom he had contact. His travels took him to South Africa and Burundi. Six received an unconfirmed report that he had crossed the border into Zamboro but they were unable to prove it. He returned the following year and this time spent a few days in Victoria.

"On neither occasion did he declare the excursions. But on the second one, we were able to confirm his presence. Naturally, we were aware that he was undertaking these journeys without the CIA's knowledge. We were preparing a report for Langley when we intercepted a phone call between Jaxom and a Zamboran official in the Ministry of the Interior. This, we felt, was the nail in the coffin—exactly the sort of information that should be relayed to Washington immediately. So we reported it up the chain."

Bull paused, meditating on the table-top before continuing.

"Then the word came back from the top floor. Downing Street had intervened. Number Ten was adamant. Under no circumstance was our report about Jaxom's indiscretions to be presented to Langley. None."

"Why?" Melissa wrinkled her nose.

"Jaxom's wife." Bull sighed. "Marianne Delgado. Daughter of Andrew Delgado…"

"The American senator," Todd finished for him. "Head of their Armed Services Committee in Congress, if I am not mistaken."

"That's him," Bull said, mouth firming in frustration. "We can't report this to our allies under pain of sanction from Number Ten. But we have no choice but to proceed as if the CIA's station in Hong Kong is compromised. You won't be contacting or receiving mission support from them. Under no circumstances are operational details of your mission to be discussed with or disclosed to our American allies."

"A sensible precaution," Todd said. "Since we're fairly sure Kasinga is in bed with Beijing. If Jaxom is working with their government, we can be reasonably assured he's either a Chinese double-agent. Or worse."

"And since this mission involves a data dump of communications between Victoria and Chinese corporate and government officials, chances are that Jaxom is aware of it. We can't afford to take any chances."

"So, what's the play?" Melissa asked.

"You're to travel east. To Macau." Bull opened another folder. "We have arranged limited support through our allies in the Portuguese intelligence service. Under a pretext, of course. With complete opaqueness where operations are concerned. We know the data drive containing the information we need is in Shīzi's hands. Top floor wants it back. At any price. You leave in four hours."

CHAPTER THIRTY-TWO

MACAU—1014 HRS (GMT +8)

Todd and Melissa flew into Macau International Airport aboard an AirAsia 737. They traveled under separate covers, sitting in different sections of the aircraft and affecting not to know one another whenever their paths crossed. Upon landing, the 737 slowed and then taxied to the main terminal building across a wide causeway separating two reservoirs. Todd's passport identified him as a Dutch industrialist arriving on a business trip. Melissa's cover was as a Scottish woman coming to attend a funeral. They were separated by a dozen passengers as they waited in line for the customs check. Once through, they reconnected in the main arrivals lobby.

"Welcome to Macau," said Melissa, glancing around. "I wonder if there's any place around here where a girl can find a Hershey bar?"

"Well, they say Macau's gambling industry is seven times that of Las Vegas," Todd replied. "I'm sure there's a place, somewhere in amongst the roulette wheels and poker chips, to buy sweets."

"There better be," Melissa grumbled. "I'm down to my last lollypop."

They had arranged to meet their Portuguese intelligence contacts at a coffee shop in the city. Todd hailed a cab and they got in. The driver's broken English was sufficient to understand the address Melissa gave and they were soon off, following a highway into the tall towers of downtown proper.

The driver dropped them off on a street corner packed with ultra-modern boutiques and restaurants. The coffee shop, which resembled a modern Starbucks, was identified with a name in Chinese ideograms that Todd could not read. Stepping through the glass-walled vestibule onto the shop floor, he recognized the soulless and sterile interior of beige tile, brown-toned décor and gleaming stainless-steel counters that was the ubiquitous face of modern corporate coffee shops worldwide. Melissa's eyes glowed as she surveyed the selection of goodies behind the counter window.

"There's your chocolate," Todd said, gesturing. Melissa ordered a huge muffin and a tea. Todd had coffee.

Their contacts arrived soon after they took seats at a table in back. The door chimed and voices alerted Todd. A young Chinese man and woman entered—university students by the looks of them, and they had evidently decided to play it as if he and Melissa were long-lost friends.

"Hello!" exclaimed the woman, a slender, bespectacled creature with long hair. "So nice to see you again!" She leaned in and gave Melissa a hug.

"What a pleasure!" The young man pumped Todd's hand enthusiastically. "It's been a long time!"

"It has," Todd agreed, smiling. The young man sported a shaved head, a mole on his cheek, and the broadest smile Todd had ever seen. Like the girl, he carried a backpack slung over one shoulder. After obtaining drinks, they sat and lowered their voices to introduce themselves.

"Welcome to Macau, Mr. Todd and Ms. Long-shanks," the man said. "My name is Yuze. And this is my twin sister Yimo."

"We appreciate your coming to meet us," said Todd. "What have you been told about our purpose here?"

"Only that we are to help you," replied Yimo with a shrug. "We are under instructions to offer every hospitality."

"And not ask too many questions," her brother added with a chuckle. "How can we be of service?"

Todd was already pleased. He was certain he was going to like working with them.

———

Yuze and Yimo ran their operation out of the small apartment downtown they shared under the guise of being humble university students. They convened in the living room, circling the coffee table to hammer out details.

"We'll need your help getting into Hong Kong," Todd explained. "We could have obtained cover that would have allowed us to fly there directly, but our service has decided to exercise extreme caution in this instance. We must enter the city anonymously."

"We have provided this service before." Yuze's voice

swelled with satisfaction. "This is, for us, a very small request. And one easily granted."

"Will you need equipment? Supplies?" Yimo asked.

"We will." Todd laid a sheet of notebook paper on the table. "These items should be sufficient."

Yuze took up the list and studied it. "We should be able to provide you with most of these items," he said. "There are a few that are beyond our capability. Perhaps we could contact our CIA friends and request their help?"

"Best not to," Melissa said. "The fewer people who know, the better."

Nods all around the table. Todd sighed in relief.

More troublesome questions avoided, he thought.

"How do you exfil people into Hong Kong?" he asked. "By boat?"

"Oh, no." Yuze shook his head. "We let the Chinese help us."

"Excuse me. The...*Chinese?*" Melissa wrinkled her nose and dug a candy bar from her purse.

Yimo laughed. "Yes! We utilize Chinese communist generosity and employ their own equipment against them. *With* their cooperation."

"How?"

"We take the bridge," Yuze chuckled. "The Hong Kong-Zhuhai-Macau Bridge. It's 55 kilometers long, spans two channels and an estuary and is our best and safest route in and out of both Hong Kong and mainland China."

"You operate in mainland China?" Todd was impressed.

Yimo was nodding. "When necessary. But in this case, we will take the bridge in the opposite direction.

There are some checkpoints along the way, but these can be negotiated."

"It's quite safe," Yuze assured them. "We have assisted agents from allied intelligence services this way in the past. We have a system that works quite well. We will bring you across concealed in a motor vehicle. Yimo and I will present our student ID cards and claim we are visiting HK to conduct research for university. The police and customs officials are generally supportive and cooperative."

Todd, aware of the great respect accorded to university students in Chinese culture, thought it a good plan.

"Come." Yuze clapped his hands. "Let us get your equipment sorted and then make preparations to travel."

CHAPTER THIRTY-THREE

MACAU / HONG KONG—1814 HRS (GMT +8)

Their journey from Macau would take place onboard Yuze and Yimo's refurbished VW microbus. It was the sort of vehicle that was a common sight during the hippie heyday of the 1960s. But instead of flower decals and peace stickers, theirs was clean and buffed to a high gloss. Two bumper stickers adorned the rear bumper: a Chinese flag and an image of the current Chinese president flashing a friendly smile and a thumbs-up.

"Nice touches," Todd said, tapping the bumper.

Yuze laughed. "Yes. To the authorities, we are just simple, patriotic, pro-China students."

"And what about us?"

"Let me show you!"

Yuze dragged open the panel door and stepped inside. The van had two rows of seats behind the driver's seat. Yuze produced a small black rectangle that resembled a car fob and clicked a button. The middle seat tilted backward to reveal an empty rectangular space large enough to hold an adult person.

"The seats are held in place by industrial strength magnets," Yuze explained. "Casual examination reveals chairs that appear welded to their base." He tapped the side of the container. "These are treated with a chemical compound that throws off sniffer dogs. We have been stopped and searched so many times that authorities know us now on sight and do not bother anymore."

"So we climb in there and you drive us across?"

"Yes."

Todd nodded. Two sets of seats, with a container each for him and Melissa. It seemed a good plan.

"I feel like bloody Dracula," Melissa groused as she lowered herself ponderously into her travel bin.

"At least you'll be safe from sunlight," Todd quipped, stepping into his own. He noted the space came equipped with a miniature light fixture and a shelf to stow small items. It was, where smuggling was concerned, comparatively luxurious. He settled in comfortably and watched as Yuze lowered the seat and darkness swallowed him.

They set out before lunch. The VW's suspension was robust and the ride, surprisingly smooth. Todd sensed their progress through the streets of Macau, speeding up and slowing as traffic demanded and occasionally stopping for lights. After a time, they came to a stop and the engine switched off. Todd's cellphone chimed with a text from Yimo.

> At the bridge. They are checking
> our travel passes.

It took over an hour for them to get underway again. Locked in his insulated steel coffin, Todd could hear nothing but could imagine the exchange of documents and answering of questions. Although he could not see out, he had studied images of the bridge and was aware of its the spans, periodic tunnels, and artificial islands that made up its length. He did his best to reckon their progress in his mind's eye. After a while, he gave up and dozed. He was roused from his nap by the sound of the magnets decoupling. Soon he was greeted by the sight of Yuze grinning down at him from above.

"Welcome to Hong Kong," he said cheerfully.

———

The packed and crowded streets of the old British enclave sweltered in the afternoon heat. Todd studied the passing faces from the door of the indoor parking garage where Yuze had parked and released them from confinement.

"Here are the keys to the apartment." Yuze handed them over. "The building is just one block from here. It is a run-down and nondescript place — hardly the sort surveilled or searched by police. You will find a Nissan with tinted windows in the parking area out back. The supplies you requested are stowed in the trunk, delivered last night by one of our colleagues."

"You work fast," said Todd, impressed.

"Thank you." Yuze smiled. "I caution you, as Westerners, to avoid even casual contact with the police. And there are plenty of them roaming the streets. They routinely stop foreigners to check passports and travel permits."

"We'll be careful," Melissa promised. She looked

fresh and rested after the trip. Todd suspected she had slept for most of the journey.

"Contact us if you need anything, or if we can be of further help," said Yimo.

They thanked the Portuguese agents and walked out to the sidewalk, melting into the crowd. They maintained a distance, never far enough to lose sight of one another but never close enough to be connected by the casual observer. They made good progress toward the apartment until reaching the intersection.

The police officer across the street was composing a traffic ticket when he paused, looked up, and saw Todd. Todd felt the man's attention zero in on him like a laser beam and knew his goose was cooked. The moment he got within range, he would be stopped and his travel documents checked. He didn't have any. So this was going to be tricky.

The light changed and Todd crossed the street, casually slipping toward the opposite side of the crosswalk from the cop, making it look like he was being jostled there by the crowd. But it was sufficient only to prompt a delay. The cop had switched course to intercept him. They would make contact in seconds.

He stepped onto the sidewalk and made as if to continue down the street when the policeman touched his arm.

"One moment, please," he said in heavily accented but perfect English. "You are a visitor to Hong Kong?"

Todd stopped, shook his head, and affected not to know English.

The cop made a book-opening gesture with his two palms, his meaning unmistakable. *Passport.* Todd drew in a deep breath, smiled, nodded, and began patting his pockets...

Melissa screamed.

Both he and the cop turned. Melissa, long hair flying and heavy body flailing, was swinging her purse at a teenage boy with a skateboard and cursing him out in fluent French. The cop paused his interrogation of Todd and immediately broke off to intervene. Todd took the opportunity to slip away into the crowd. When he crossed the street to gain line of sight on Melissa, she was gone.

He found her again, sitting on the apartment steps, munching on a candy bar.

"How did you manage to slip away?" he asked, genuinely puzzled.

She grinned. "I may be big, luv, but I'm fast. Care for a lollypop?"

CHAPTER THIRTY-FOUR

HONG KONG—1622 HRS (GMT +8)

Internet access proved an unexpected challenge.

"Bloody Chinese firewalls!" Melissa groaned, slamming her fist on the kitchen table of the small apartment safehouse they were using. Todd stepped over and peered at the screen of her laptop. She had three tabs open on her browser, one for each of the main three search engines available via Chinese state internet: Baidu, Sogou, and Haosou. Accessing certain streams of data required the entering of personal data and account passwords.

"My, they *do* control access to information here, don't they?" He smirked. "You can circumvent it with TidalRip."

He drew up a chair and sat beside Melissa as she accessed the GCHQ-provided encryption software used to bypass firewalls and facilitate secret communications from agents in the field. With a few clicks, they had cleared their way to unintercepted net access.

"Here we go!" She hit <ENTER> and the browser screen cleared to reveal the gleaming towers and concrete buttresses of the Shīzi building in downtown Hong Kong. "Shīzi Global corporate headquarters. And!" She waggled her eyebrows meaningfully. "Where our good pal Mr. Shīzi maintains his private offices."

Todd studied the building. It was a damned fortress!

"Well…" He scratched his chin. "First things first. We should arrange surveillance on the comings and goings to and from the building. Try to get a fix on exactly where Shīzi has his desk. And anything else we can find out."

"We have Falconets," she said. "Yuze and Yimo were able to access six."

"More than we'll need." Todd grinned. The miniature Falconet surveillance cameras, about the size of marbles, had pan-tilt-zoom capability and NASA-level optics. Placing them at vantage points capable of monitoring critical areas would be a fairly simple matter. "We can upload the footage here and speed through the boring bits. Are we online with the facial recognition software?"

"Got it here." She tapped the hard drive. "We have a complete database of known Chinese political and intelligence operatives. We'll gain a harvest of useful intel, no problem."

"Alright then." He sat back and crossed his arms. "Now to figure out how to get the cameras where they need to be."

"Both there and at Shīzi's home." She puffed out her cheeks with a sigh. "Wherever that is."

He nodded. "One thing at a time. Once we know

his routine, we can arrange to shadow him to his house and place cameras there, as well."

"We have our work cut out for us!"

"Don't we always?"

———

2011 HRS (GMT +8)

They began placing Falconets around Shīzi Towers later that night.

The streets of Hong Kong never slept. There was a steady stream of traffic and pedestrians in the streets around the safe house. But as they left downtown and headed for the business district where their target lay, traffic thinned. Here the properties were larger, more like the office plazas and complexes Todd associated with the US and UK. The Shīzi Towers complex lay on a broad boulevard of other office and retail buildings. Given the time of night, pedestrians were scarce.

No place to blend in, Todd thought. *I'll have to improvise.*

"Right," he said. "Drop me here opposite the main entrance. I'll reconnoiter and place some cameras while you circle the block."

"Right. Will do." She slowed, stopped and allowed him to exit the passenger side before continuing on.

A white man alone on the street in Hong Kong at this hour would stick out like a sore thumb. That was uppermost on Todd's mind as he looked around, orienting himself. He wanted to get close enough to the entrance to assess the security presence and place a camera by the door. So he used the tried and tested technique of simple acting like he belonged there. In his trousers and jacket, he resembled a western business-man. Why wouldn't such a person have business here? So he hiked the walkway to the main doors.

The building was darkened, but a light shone in the lobby. Luck was with him. The security officer at the main desk rose just as Todd arrived and left to do his rounds. Todd peered through the glass door and was satisfied the guard was alone. He placed a Falconet on the lintel by the door just above eye level. The camouflage feature of the unit caused the glass camera's skin to automatically blend with the lintel's background color. With any luck, no one would spot or question its presence there for a day or so.

He only missed the police car by a few seconds.

He was just stepping onto the curb when he saw a pair of headlights preparing to round the corner and head in his direction. He flung himself to the sidewalk, hugging the cement beside a parked car.

Can't be Melissa. Not this fast, he thought. *Christ, I hope they didn't see me...*

His prudence was warranted. As he lay prone. The car slowed and a searchlight beamed toward the entrance of the Shīzi building. From Todd's vantage point, he could just make out the entrance. The guard appeared in the lit square of the doorway and waved. The searchlight clicked off and the car pulled forward. Only then did Todd see the roof lights and distinct markings of the Hong Kong Police Force.

He let out a long, slow, ragged exhale.

Melissa came along about a minute later. By then he was back on his feet and had a hand out for the passenger door handle. As casually as he could, he opened it and slipped back inside.

"Once more around the block," he said. "And I'll set some up across the street so we can track cars."

"Like the rozzers who just went by?" Melissa shook her head. "That was a close shave."

"Bloody right!"

CHAPTER THIRTY-FIVE

HONG KONG—2148 HRS (GMT +8)

Shīzi's residence was located in the Peak residential neighborhood. Easily Hong Kong's most expensive real estate market, the Peak had been all but been forbidden to Chinese residents. The colonial oligarchs—the nouveau merchant nobility, fallen aristocrats, and remittance men—had been carried up and down from their summer residences on sedan chairs by coolies. Boasting sumptuous mansions with whimsical names like the Union Arms and Dun Roman, the tree-lined streets of the Peak were like a still pond in the gentle Hong Kong night.

If police cruisers make random stops by Shīzi's office, how much more likely are they to patrol his residential neighborhood? Todd wondered. He reckoned the odds as highly likely.

"Here we go," murmured Melissa, guiding the Nissan down the narrow, winding streets of what housing experts worldwide agreed was the least affordable housing market in the world. The neighbor-hood was schizophrenic, with the narrow white mono-liths of uber-modern designer luxury homes packed cheek-by-jowl with the rolling estates of large colonial mansions. Shīzi lived tucked away in one of the most remote.

Thoroughfare Gap Road was a thumb-shaped cul-de-sac that jutted out from a main artery like Caesar's digit at the games. Three driveways extended from the road, the largest gated and electronically monitored.

"We'll have to knock that out." Todd pointed at the CCTV camera on the stone lintels supporting the wrought-iron gate.

Melissa peered up through the windshield. The surveillance camera was a flat black rectangle with a gleaming red light inset beside its lens. The rectangle was mounted on a bracket and a pair of twisted wires trailed from its back into an aperture inset in the lintel.

"Standard analog surveillance camera. 1980s tech-nology." She sniffed. "You'd think Shīzi would have better equipment."

"He's a frugal man."

"Well, all right then." She sighed and produced her cellphone. Swiping to the main screen she summoned an app and punched a few buttons. The glowing red light on the camera went out.

Todd slipped from the vehicle and placed Falconets on the lintel and at a vantage point low on the curb across the street which granted them a wide-angle shot of the gate. The adaptive skin of the Falconets each changed color to blend into the background behind them. Satisfied, Todd looked both ways, crossed the street and let himself back into the Nissan's passenger's seat.

"Let's swing back by the office building and place one or two more. Then head home."

"Fine," said Melissa. "We've done a good night's work. No need to push our luck."

———

They returned to the safehouse and managed a digital link with the feed of each Falconet. The livestream began, with images fed into the facial recognition database of Chinese intelligence personnel. Then they had a bite to eat and lay down for the night.

It seemed to Todd as if he had just closed his eyes when he was suddenly awakened by someone shaking his arm.

"Dickie." It was Melissa. "Wakey-wakey, sport."

Instantly he snapped to, both eyes opening, a deep breath drawn and then he was sitting upright on the couch where he'd spend the night. "What's up?" he asked around a yawn.

"It's just past 6 AM, Dickie old sport." Melissa, in a t-shirt and spandex pants, stood there clutching a cup of coffee. "Just past dawn and we've already hit paydirt."

He rose and followed her to where the laptop sat open on the kitchen table. The window for the Falconet livestream was up, but a red light blinked alongside a red number 5 in the upper right-hand corner.

"Five hits," she said. "That's five Chinese spies in and out of Shīzi's office as logged by the facial recognition software."

Todd let out a low whistle. "So they're in and out of the building at all hours?"

"It would appear so." She sat and began toggling

buttons. "That explains the special police courtesy patrol and the guard at the desk. But whatever's in there is something important enough to send these guys. *Voila!*"

With a keystroke she brought up a panel of black and white images: digital intercepts of Chinese intelligence service official ID photos. Alongside each was a rectangle of information in Chinese ideograms. Todd watched as the letters swam, then became blue before reappearing in English per the translation software.

"Special action service branch of Chinese state security," Melissa breathed. "That's the hard team. The heavy brigade. Whatever Shīzi's got in that building, it's important enough to send the cream of the crop of Chinese intelligence to guard it."

"So, we can assume the data drive is there. Probably in his office. But not *just* the data drive. Likely additional documentation and correspondence on his office computer. Perhaps some hardware or other technology in a secure storage unit. With those boys involved, it could be anything."

He studied the faces on the screen. Every operative had short hair, a square jaw, a cruel face, and lively intelligence dancing in the eyes. The most dangerous kind of wolves. Counterintelligence specialists, authorized by the Chinese state to kill its enemies at will. Having them roaming the streets was like unleashing a Navy SEAL or SAS team on the civilian guests at a holiday resort.

"It will be the diamonds." Melissa said these words flatly, tonelessly.

"Go on…"

"Sir Arnold briefed Six about the diamond fields

there. That's got to be the big lure for Shīzi...*and* the Chinese government."

"You're thinking they're working hand-in-glove to get China a seat at the table in the global diamond market."

"It would do wonders for their currency troubles," Melissa said. Then, in answer to Todd's look of curiosity added, "London School of Economics, luv. Took some night classes. Did you know Mick Jagger went there, too?"

CHAPTER THIRTY-SIX

HONG KONG—1237 HRS (GMT +8)

Over the next few hours, more notifications streamed in from the facial recognition database. Visitors from both the Chinese government and security services were frequent guests at both Shīzi's home and office. They came and went seemingly at all hours of the day and night. Todd began wondering about the extent to which Shīzi was a free agent or an asset being held under close protection and observation by a government riding the back of his power and influence to advance geopolitical goals.

"Protection," Melissa said when he asked her thoughts on the matter. "They're guarding him. And, by extension, whatever negotiations he currently has underway with Kasinga's government."

"The private sector as a wedge to further the goals of the Chinese Communist Party is a common MO in our day and age," Todd admitted. Chinese NGOs accounted for much of the nation's footprint in Africa.

"This diamond venture is being seen as a very big deal, then."

"I'm thinking the data drive is in the office," she affirmed.

"Either that or he carries it around with him." He peered over her shoulder at the laptop's screen. "Any word from Yuze and Yimo on that request we sent?"

Melissa clicked over to the encrypted e-mail window and scanned her inbox. "Here we are!" she said brightly, clicking on a message. "Let's see... Yes. They've affirmed the items have been secured and are on route."

"Good," Todd said. He had begun to formulate a plan.

———

Paper was a major lifeblood of Hong Kong—or, at least, one of them. Like every single city in the world that played host to massive multinationals, HK had its own supply of shredding services, not the least of which was Jueh.

Jueh was the termite of the Chinese business world. While other shredding companies dispatched cumbersome trucks to negotiate the winding streets of Hong Kong, Jueh employed a fleet of cleverly-adapted scooters that whisked in and out of traffic, collecting and removing the strips of shredded paper that were the excretion of every major corporate office in town. Jueh reps were afforded a great deal of deference in traffic, even by the police who routinely waved through their couriers while holding other vehicles back.

Jueh drivers wore a visored helmet, keeping it on even during pick-ups and deliveries.

———

The package arrived from Macau in the afternoon. A courier stopped by their safehouse, offered a sheet for signature, and departed without even making eye contact. Todd brought the rectangular package back to the kitchen table.

"What's this, then?" Melissa asked, eyeing it over the rim of her teacup.

Todd smirked and slitted open the box, producing two documents and a small wooden case.

"Tourist passes. And fake rental documents for the Nissan." He laid these before her.

"And that?" She tipped her chin at the case.

Todd opened it, revealing a gleaming silver pistol about the size of a compact automatic. But instead of bullets, the twin magazines held what appeared to be flechette or darts of some kind.

"Oh, Dickie." She began chuckling. "You're a wicked boy, aren't you?"

———

The Jueh scooter passed by the mouth of the alley every day at 2 PM.

It was not the sort of thing he'd noticed as an operational necessity. It was rather one of the annoying details of safehouse life he had come to register as a flicker in his subconscious such that he noticed every time the courier floated past. But now it had become useful. It was funny how things turned out.

Todd waited around the corner of the alley as the mosquito buzz of the scooter approached. He's reckoned the speed at not more than thirty kilometers per hour. He'd paced off the distance so now closed his eyes and counted. At ten he stepped out from around the corner, raised the silver pistol, and fired. The flechette hit the driver dead center in his chest. His mouth gaped and he peered down at the dart protruding from his windbreaker, then abruptly lost consciousness. The scooter veered left and collided with the curb. No sooner had the driver spilled over than Todd was out of the alley, dragging him in behind the dumpster, then returning to fetch the bike.

———

"Charming, Dickie. You look absolutely spiffing in that uniform."

Todd stood before the hallway mirror, examining his image. The uniform was too small for him and his arms dangled out of the sleeves. But he could cheat that. It was the pants that were causing him grief. The hem stopped several inches shy of his ankle.

"Wish I had a set of puttees," he said.

"Here." Melissa knelt beside him. "Used to work with a bloke who wore his pants like this…"

Todd watched as she hiked up his socks, tucked the hem of his pants inside, and puffed out the bottoms bell-bottom style.

"Jump style?" Todd frowned, his eyes and nose invisible behind the Jueh helmet visor.

"People do it sometimes," Melissa said.

"Misguided military geeks in search of attention." Todd sighed. "Do you honestly think there's a Jueh courier anywhere here in Hong Kong who's that much of an individualist to buck style trends?"

"You'd be the first, Dickie."

"How's our guest?"

Melissa turned to the Jueh courier, who was out cold on the couch and handcuffed to its base for good measure. "I can keep him under safely for another thirty-six hours. Any longer, it becomes dangerous. Too many toxins in the bloodstream."

"We'll be done long before then." Todd pulled off the helmet and went into his room to change back into his normal clothes. The bike and courier were safely stowed. Only a few final details to work out before they moved against the office complex. Everything depended on split-second timing.

And a bloody silly way to wear my pants, he thought. But it was the least of their challenges.

CHAPTER THIRTY-SEVEN

To Todd's surprise, Melissa managed to fish out a pattern in the comings and goings of Chinese intelligence personnel.

"They seem to follow a schedule," she said, scrolling through Falconet footage. "Took me a while, but I began to notice... Between two and three AM, six of them arrive in fifteen-minute intervals, entering by separate doors. That struck me as significant. So I scrolled back and noticed that between midnight and one AM, six others leave. And they take no particular care to hide it."

"Shift change!" Todd laughed. "So, one shift ends at midnight and another starts at 2 AM. The two-hour window allows them to infil and exfil their staff with sufficient time between arrivals to avoid arousing suspicion." He shook his head. "Clever."

"But not as clever as me!"

"Keep up this good work, and I'll have the King buy you a pound of chocolate."

"Ooh! Swiss, please…"

———

They needed to get Falconets inside the building. Todd's infiltration tonight was intended to do just that, as well as get a sense of where Shīzi kept his office. Melissa had some clues for him before he set out.

"I've been able to get a partial shot of the elevator from the front door," she said. "An awful lot of activity seems to center on the fifth floor."

"Interesting." Now dressed in his Jueh courier gear, helmet under one arm, he studied the CCTV images. The elevator door and overhead floor indicator panel was just visible if she tilted and zoomed the micro-cam sufficiently toward the image. Following the arriving agents entering at their staggered fifteen-minute intervals, she had been able to confirm that each one entered and took an elevator to the fifth floor. "I'll see about putting a Falconet into the elevator car, as well."

"Good luck, Dickie." She sat back and shook her head. "And be careful."

———

He timed his departure such that he would arrive at the Shīzi building between 1:15 and 1:45 AM, judging that to be the time when security coverage would be thinnest. He planned to approach openly and attempt to bluff his way into the building. He judged that he had less than a fifty percent chance of making it inside and so brought along the silver tranquillizer pistol. If any meeting looked likely to involve more than he and one other person, he would use it and make his getaway.

He guided the scooter through the silent streets of the business district. The black monolith of the Shīzi building loomed ahead. He drew a deep breath, turned and steered toward the lit square of the main entrance. A lone security guard sat on duty behind the reception desk. Todd brought the scooter to a halt a dozen yards from the door, kicked down the stand and approached, keeping his helmet on as he had seen other drivers do.

Now we'll see how the guard reacts, Todd thought.

He drew a deep breath and approached the door with the bag for shredded documents slung over his shoulder.

To his surprise, the guard simply rose from the desk, unlocked the door, and let him in wordlessly. Todd made for the elevator, the muscles at the base of his spine knotted against a sudden cry or gunshot. But neither came. When he reached the elevator, he turned back to see the guard back in his place at the desk, his attention on the comic book in his hands.

Todd boarded the elevator and touched the button for the fifth floor.

———

The door slid open on a dark corridor.

Todd stepped out onto a wine-red carpet in a narrow hallway. There were closed office doors along either side and no sign of people. He noted the corridor widened ahead to his right, so he struck off in that direction, pausing to test random doors as he went. All were unlocked, reassuring him that he had places to take refuge if necessary.

The corridor broadened into a wide reception area. A large round reception station sat in the middle of the space before a wide double door flanked by ornate brass lions fashioned in the Chinese style, with square heads and lolling tongues.

X marks the spot, he thought, remembering that Shīzi, in Chinese, meant lion.

He crossed the reception area quickly and tried the double doors.

Locked.

He fished a Falconet from his pocket and placed it on the rear of one of the lions, the micro-camera changing color to blend in with its brass backing. That position would provide footage of everyone coming in and out of the office. Todd was getting set to place another one when he heard voices.

The elevator door rumbled down the hall and he knew he was trapped. Two men were approaching. With a glance, Todd verified them as young, muscular types in identical black suits. *Chinese intelligence,* he thought. He would look damned suspicious ducking into one of the offices ahead of them. So he drew the silver pistol out and gripped it, concealing his right hand inside the courier bag while grappling with the receptionist's portable shredder with his left. By the time the two men entered the reception area, he was dragging out fistfuls of shredded paper and pushing them into the bag.

The two men walked past without giving him so much as a glance.

He exited through the lobby, the guard glancing up from his comic book only briefly as he passed by. Todd let himself out, boarded the scooter, and buzzed off down the path toward the street and back to the safehouse. Melissa, seated at the kitchen table with the laptop, was jubilant.

"Well done, Dickie," she said. "We have a strong feed from the Falconet by Shīzi's office and it's perfectly placed."

"Glad to hear it." He sighed and sank into a chair. "It was touch and go, but I made it in and out. And nobody said a word."

"Luck's still on our side."

"Let's hope it sticks around."

CHAPTER THIRTY-EIGHT

They made the decision to breach Shīzi's office at the same time the following morning.

"Now that the pattern has been set of Jueh couriers arriving in the wee hours, we should take advantage of it," he said. "My guess is that Shīzi's office is on a separate alarm system."

Melissa nodded. "Neutralizing that and forcing the lock should be no problem." She checked her notes. "Shīzi came to work this morning at ten and entered his office. Hasn't been seen since."

"He may have a separate exit," Todd suggested. "We know the Chinese intelligence traffic in and out of the building is minimal between one and two AM. So it should be safe for us to have a second unit—you—in place."

"What's the plan?"

Todd thought for a moment. "We'll go in tandem, me on the scooter and you in the Nissan. You post up a block or so away while I go in. I suspect I'll be coming out fast, either on foot or via scooter. Once we link up, we'll ditch the scooter and uniform and make our getaway."

"Hopefully you'll find the drive." She sighed. "Because after this, if you want to go in again, you'll have to find another ruse."

"One ruse at a time, luv."

They turned and examined the unconscious courier on the couch.

"What shall we do with him?"

Todd shrugged. "Douse him with booze and drop him off in an alley somewhere."

———

After doing just that, they made their way toward the target.

"There's the tower," Melissa's voice said in his ear. "Turning off now."

"Got it." Todd squinted through the visor of his courier helmet at the monolithic office building rising ahead. The streets around it were quiet at this hour, and he reckoned his chances at success as excellent.

Job one was to reclaim the data drive. But, failing that, Todd was equipped with another piece of TidalRip kit he and Melissa had brought with them. The Ajax data worm was installed on a drive in his hip pocket. Inserted into a port on Shīzi's desktop computer, the drive would take only a few seconds to install the encrypted software on the hard-drive. Once there, the worm could be accessed remotely, offering them an inside track into Shīzi's business PC.

If we can't grab the drive, then we can at least neutralize its contents the next time he inserts it, he thought. Not the preferred outcome, but it would do in a pinch.

The lobby appeared ahead, the guard at his desk. Todd drove up, parked, and was again admitted wordlessly by the guard. He took the elevator to the fifth floor.

It was deserted, as it had been last night, and there was no sign of the Chinese intelligence operatives. Todd quickly made his way down the hall to the reception hub, knelt, and began rummaging through the receptionist's shredder, using the time to scan the area. There was no sight, no sound, no smell of anyone else's presence so he rose and stepped over to the main office door between the two brass dragons.

There was no outward sign of an alarm system, but he wasn't about to take any chances. He pulled his cell phone from a pocket, called up the EMP app, and directed a mini-burst at the door. The pulse would temporarily disable electronic signals from any devices that might be attached. That done, he attacked the lock.

"Tíngzhǐ!"

The voice cracked out from behind him. Todd paused, raised his hands, and turned slowly.

It was the guard from the lobby. How he had come to be on this floor was a mystery to Todd. *Perhaps he used the stairs?* But there was no denying he stood not a dozen yards away, arm raised, a look of alarm on his face. Todd cocked his head and waited.

The guard began questioning him in Chinese. Todd stood and listened, waiting for a prompt to respond. Todd didn't speak Chinese and that would soon become obvious. At some point, it would dawn on the unarmed guard that he was not responding normally. But the man was voluble, snapping a series of angry statements that ended in what was obviously a question. Todd nodded, lowered his hands, and made calming gestures. *Wait, wait just a minute,* his hands were saying in the international language of the cautious, the scared, of those caught by surprise.

The guard snapped again, repeating his question. Todd nodded and reached for his pocket.

"Tíngzhǐ!" the guard cried again, hand scrabbling for his radio.

Todd's fist sprang from his pocket holding the silver tranquillizer pistol. *Fft!* A flechette hit the guard, dead center of his chest. His eyes widened in surprise and he looked down. The dart, along with a thin trickle of blood, was visible on the front of his uniform shirt. He stumbled, catching himself on the edge of the receptionist's desk. His hand tightened around the radio mike...

Then he keeled over, unconscious.

Todd waited.

No movement. No sound. The guard had been patrolling alone, going about his regular sweeps, not called here by any alarm or CCTV images. He had merely stumbled upon Todd in the act and challenged him. And for that he'd paid the price.

Todd was safe.

He reapplied himself to the lock, working feverishly. Time was of the essence. And he was a little more hurried than usual, knowing this would be the last time they would breach the office tower. Soon, his efforts were rewarded: the knob clicked and the door drifted open a few inches.

Todd turned and knelt beside the guard, flipping him onto his back. Then he crouched, grabbed the unconscious body beneath the armpits, and began dragging him backwards into Shīzi's office. It was tough going because the guard, although small, was stocky and heavy. It took every ounce of effort to drag him across the threshold and onto the gold carpet of the sumptuous executive suite. Todd dragged him across the threshold, stepped over him, and shut the door with a sigh of relief. He turned.

It was a gorgeous office. Two large plate glass windows looked out over the lights of Hong Kong. Modern office furniture alternated with priceless Chinese art objects. A set of stout bookshelves lined the far wall beside another door sporting titles in English, Chinese, French, and Russian. And across the executive desk, next to its computer, slumped Shīzi, a bullet hole in his temple.

CHAPTER THIRTY-NINE

Todd allowed himself two complete breaths to take in the sight before getting to work.

He moved in close, probing the Chinese billionaire's pulse with a fingertip to the neck. Even before pressing far enough in to reach an artery, he knew the truth; the flesh was as cool as porcelain and his form had that weird, shrunken quality Todd had come to know from battlefields and operational scenarios across the world. There could be no doubt whatsoever that Shīzi was as dead as the proverbial door nail.

He glanced over at the guard. The man lay prone, the tranq having taken full effect. He would be out for several hours.

Nevertheless, Todd moved quickly. Reaching into a pocket, he produced his cell phone and connected it to a port via a shielded wire. With the push of a button, he kicked the Ajax data worm into motion. During the few seconds it took to download to the data drive, he scanned Shīzi's desk. And noticed something clutched in the man's fingers.

It's the cap of the data drive. Shīzi must have been here in his office, connecting the drive to his computer when his mysterious guest had appeared and…

There was something about the placement of the bullet, about the precision and care with which it had been positioned. This was the work of a top-level professional. There were only a handful of such men in the world.

And one managed to find his way up here, make it through the security gauntlet, and do this.

His cell phone beeped, informing him the download was complete. It was time to get the hell out of here.

Todd went to the door and peeked out into the reception area. *Empty.* Luck was still with him. He edged out, closing the door softly behind him. He saw no sign of anyone in the hallway. He bent to the receptionist's shredder, manhandled the scraps into his bag, rose, and made for the elevator. As he stood waiting for it to arrive, he noted the panel for the car beside it flickering. Someone was going up and stopping, floor by floor…

It could be the intelligence crew, searching for the guard.

Todd turned from the elevator, pushed the crush bar of the fire exit door, and emerged onto the landing of the stairs. Taking them two at a time, he descended to the lobby.

His spy's sixth sense was pinning the red end of the dial. Something was wrong. He could feel it instinctively, and years of service with the Royal Marines and MI-6 had taught him to pay close attention to his instincts. Arriving on the ground floor, he paused by the fire door and waited, listening. Far above him, he heard the crash of another door opening and closing. They were searching the stairwell.

He opened the door and crack and peeked out into the lobby.

Two of the Chinese intelligence operatives were standing by the guard stations, tinkering with the computer. Whatever they were trying to do there wasn't working because he could see their frustration. *Trying to access the CCTV cameras?* he wondered. It seemed likely. They probably counted on the guard to monitor the CCTV while they patrolled other areas of the building. As he watched, one of the intelligence agents left the desk and took an elevator up, leaving one man by himself at the guard's desk.

Todd took a deep breath, pushed through the door, and sauntered toward the entrance.

The agent at the desk looked up and spoke. Todd waved and continued walking.

The agent spoke again, this time in a menacing tone. Todd pretended not to hear him and reached for the door…

And then the spy was up and moving toward him, barking orders. Todd imagined the effect on the average Chinese citizen would be dramatic. But he merely stepped out and made for the Jueh scooter resting on its stand. He swung a leg over as the agent burst through the door, waving his hands and calling.

Inside, he saw elevator doors opening and agents pouring into the lobby.

Todd kicked the scooter to life, steered clear of the agent's attempts to intercept him, and made for the road.

He could hear yelling behind him, the sound of doors banging open. He glanced over his shoulder. The agents had spilled out onto the walkway. Some had cell phones out while others made for vehicles. Todd grinned and gunned the little scooter. It flew down the street with a mosquito whine.

Headlights appeared in his rear view mirror—distant pinpricks of diamond white light against the night. Todd steered off the road, onto the sidewalk and down the walkway of a deserted park. The little scooter gamely buzzed along, dashing up and down the rolling cement path lined with streetlights. Todd came to a playground, ditched the scooter, tore off the courier suit covering his black clothes, and melted into the trees.

———

Melissa was waiting at the rendezvous point. Todd slid into the Nissan's passenger seat and shut the door.

"Nice day at the office, luv?" She started the car and steered toward downtown. Within minutes they were within a block or two of the safehouse.

"I bumped into Shīzi."

"Oh?" Her eyebrows jumped. "And was he pleased to see you?"

"Can't say." Todd shrugged. "He's dead. Shot through the temple. A professional job."

Melissa said nothing for a long moment. They floated down the street toward the safehouse and pulled into a parking spot by the front door. When she switched off the ignition, she finally spoke.

"Dead, you say?" She shook her head. "Well, that puts an interesting wrinkle in things, doesn't it?"

CHAPTER FORTY

Police sirens chased each other through the streets until the wee hours. Todd figured Chinese intelligence had put out an all-points-bulletin about the courier and the hounds were out in force. They were likely searching for a Chinese national—a random Jueh courier that had fled detainment by security services. But given the building in question and Shīzi's dead body lying in his office, that the involvement of foreign operatives was being considered a possibility. So they stayed put, keeping a low profile, each occupied by specific mission priorities.

Melissa engaged TidalRip and navigated her way across the internet to the Ajax worm in Shīzi's office PC. She cheerfully reported that the link was firmly established and that Shīzi had the plethora of data privileges one would expect a company owner to have in his business' own network. "I've got a way to tunnel into the building's CCTV cache," she said. "With any luck,

I'll be able to burrow deep enough to roll back footage to see who it was that topped the old boy."

Todd was pleased. The Falconet footage showed a parade of visitors in and out of the office but provided a blurry photo of the last visitor—a shadowy figure that had gone in for a 9 PM meeting and then exited an hour later. Todd was working on the assumption that this was the likely assassin. Although one could never be sure.

When Melissa took a break, he used TidalRip to initiate a secure video call with Sir Reginald Bull in London. The rumpled MI-6 lawyer looked like he had recently been put through the ringer. Bleary-eyed, tie loosened, and sweaty, he peered back at Todd through the video conference window on the desktop.

"Well, Dickie. What news?" Sir Reginald cleared his throat and gulped a swallow of water from a glass. "Any progress on getting the data drive back?"

"Shīzi is dead," Todd said flatly. "He was shot in the head at close range in his own office—in a building crawling with security. It was a professional job."

"And the data drive?"

"Gone. Although we managed to put a tap on his computer. Melissa is going through it now, both for CCTV and e-mail traffic related to the drive."

"You managed to get in and out clean, I hope?"

"No fatalities," Todd said. "Although I had to disable some guards, and a bike courier. No doubt Chinese intel are on high alert for foreign spies at this time."

"Bloody bad timing." Sir Reginald puffed out his cheeks. "The Chinese are gearing up for a summit with the Americans this week. They'll be looking for heads to put on display for the western press. Let's make sure yours isn't one of them."

"Yes, sir."

"I want you to start making plans to exfil from China." Sir Reginald sighed. "Get everything you can now and make sure GCHQ has a line on Shīzi's computer so they can get cracking on data analysis."

"Right."

———

Melissa briefed him over lunch, which was sandwiches at the kitchen table with the laptop open in front of them.

"I've got a line on our shooter," she said around a mouthful of tuna. "And some very interesting e-mail traffic."

"Let's start with the shooter." Todd moved his chair around to more clearly see the screen.

"Oh, he's top level, Dickie. Very sharp." She touched the mousepad and a video clip of an exit stairwell leapt into view. As Todd watched, a fire door opened and a man emerged onto the landing pushing a janitor's cart, wearing coveralls and a baseball cap.

"Why is the face blurred?" Todd squinted as the figure set down a backpack and began unzipping his coveralls.

"My guess is he's wearing pixelating make-up."

"Really?" Todd was impressed. Use of make-up patterns to foil CCTV and facial recognition software was a professional touch. "What's he changing into?"

"Watch."

They did, as the man on the landing transformed

himself from a building janitor into a Chinese intelligence agent, dark suit and all.

Todd whistled. "Bold as bloody brass."

Melissa hit a key and the picture switched to an interior view of Shīzi's office. "This is on a separate feed," she said. "Even building security doesn't have access. The feed leads directly to Shīzi's PC. He kept a record of his meetings."

Todd watched as Shīzi, seated at his desk, worked on his computer.

"He's writing an e-mail," Melissa explained.

"To whom?"

"We'll come to that in a minute." Her eyes twinkled. "Watch."

Shīzi suddenly paused and cocked his head. The audio feed picked up the *click* of his office door opening. The man who had changed into the dark suit and sunglasses in the stairwell appeared, entering the office and offering the billionaire a slight bow. Shīzi turned back to his computer and muttered something in Chinese. While his attention was on the screen, the man in the dark suit drew a silenced automatic from beneath his jacket with casual confidence. He raised it and a soft *thut* sounded. The bullet hole blossomed in Shīzi's temple and he slumped forward onto the desk.

The man in the dark suit stepped forward, reached down, and plucked the data drive from its port. Then he turned and left the office.

"Cool as a bloody cucumber," Todd muttered.

"The complete professional," Melissa agreed. "In and out in under twenty seconds."

Todd sighed and shook his head. They were up against a thoroughgoing pro. As if they didn't have enough problems.

"So, who was Shīzi sending an e-mail to?"

"You won't believe it."

"Try me." He smiled.

Her lips firmed. "Arnold Jaxom. The CIA's super-hacker in Hong Kong."

CHAPTER FORTY-ONE

"What?"

Todd's mind reeled with the news. He recalled Sir Reginald's admonition to not involve CIA and the briefing about Jaxom's clandestine trips to Zamboro. The webs of deception were growing so thick around this situation that it was hard to tell the forest from the trees.

But now Melissa was talking again, filling him in on the correspondence. Yes, Shīzi had been in contact with a known CIA officer—one MI-6 suspected had been compromised. But it was not as straightforward as a direct exchange.

"Jaxom has been involved with establishing CIA shell companies around the world, including here in the Far East," she said. "One in particular. It's called Blue-bird LLC and it's based in Turks & Caicos. Shīzi's conversation was ostensibly with Bluebird but the e-mail address he was corresponding with is a known cypher used by Jaxom."

"So what were they talking about?"

"I don't know." The frustration was audible in her voice. "In addition to everything else, he used a special encryption key to code and decode correspondence back and forth. I've contacted GCHQ. They've got a cryptographer working the problem."

"Alright." This was encouraging. "Sir Reginald wants us to begin making preparations to exfil as soon as possible. With the worm embedded in Shīzi's hard drive, our work here is more or less done. We'll tie up some loose ends and make arrangements to slip away in the night."

"How are you planning on doing that?"

"Same way we came in. I'll lay in a call to our friends in Macau," he said. But when he did, all he got was voicemail.

———

"Dickie, you'd better see this."

Todd turned from his laptop to see Melissa standing in the doorway of the kitchen, a worried expression on her face. He rose and followed her.

"This just broke on the Chinese news a few minutes ago." She turned the laptop on the table to face him. Onscreen was a shot of an apartment building surrounded by police vehicles. Todd's breath quickened when he recognized it as the block of flats where Yimo and Yuze had their safehouse in Macau.

"My God..." He sank into a chair, his head swimming.

"I've run what I could through translation software." She shivered and crossed her arms to steady herself. "They've been identified by name and arrested. The Portuguese ambassador has been called on the carpet. There's a general sweep underway by Chinese security forces in Macau."

Todd's mind raced. Of all the obstacles they could face under the circumstances, this was the absolute worst. Their mode of transport in and out of Hong Kong had been snatched away. They were behind the lines in enemy territory with fake tourist paperwork and no way out.

"Dickie, what are we going to do?"

"Six wants us to exfil," he said calmly. "And, impossible as it seems, that is exactly what we are going to do."

"How?"

He grinned. "I have a few ideas, luv."

———

A plan was formulating in his mind—a strategy to exfil from Hong Kong that was daring and risky—one that had, by his reckoning, a less than fifty percent chance of success. Those chances would improve greatly if they could turn their present disadvantages into assets. Some purchases would be called for.

"We have the travel passes," he told Melissa. "So we're going play that hand to the hilt." He handed over a sheet of paper. "Here."

"What's this?"

"Shopping list." Todd studied Melissa's stocky frame, her plain face, her fingertips with their light stain of chocolate on them from the last candy bar. In a sense, the woman's appearance functioned as its own best cover. "There's a department store not far from here. Take the Nissan and just blend in. A nice tourist lady out for a shop."

"Fair enough." She studied the list. "Suntan lotion…beach hats… For God's sake, Dickie. You don't actually expect me to buy a swimsuit, do you?"

"Yes. And a Hawaiian style shirt for me, please."

"I haven't worn a swimming costume since university!"

"You'll look fine. We'll also need sandals."

"What the—"

"And beach towels."

"You mad bugger! What do you have up your sleeve?"

Todd grinned and turned the screen of his laptop to her. There was a video feed of the HMS *Prince of Wales* transiting the Taiwan Strait, much to the annoyance of Beijing.

"We're going to hitch a lift," he said. And laughed.

———

His research into resorts on the coast was bearing fruit. One in particular looked like it would fit the bill. In addition to the necessary recreational facilities, it maintained a popular reputation among western tourists. Todd had not been issued cover credit cards so might be forced to resort to his own. Withdrawing money from a cash machine would be more prudent.

While Melissa was out shopping, he put the final steps of his plan into play with another video conference call to Sir Reginald. The old MI-6 lawyer was pleased to hear from him.

"Glad to see you're still upright," Sir Reginald said. "GCHQ has picked up an increase in operational tempo among the Chinese secret service in Hong Kong. They're on the lookout for foreign spies."

"I'm not surprised." Todd noted the video feed was full of news regarding Shīzi's death. "They've lost their point man in Zamboro."

"Yes. They're being poor sports about it." Sir Reginald paused. "GCHQ has been able to identify the assassin."

"And?"

"Brace yourself. It's Raptor."

Todd closed his eyes. Raptor was arguably one of the top three freelance hit men in the world and a well-known favorite of the CIA.

"So Langley was involved."

"Maybe. Maybe not. Either way, Dickie, you and Melissa need to up sticks and bugger off. The sooner the better."

"We'll move shortly," Todd replied. "I have a plan."

He suppressed his amusement as he laid out the details and watched Sir Reginald's face turn white.

CHAPTER FORTY-TWO

HONG KONG—0426 HRS (GMT +8)

They rose in the wee hours of the morning, loaded their luggage into the Nissan, then erased every trace of their presence in the safe house. Todd went through all the drawers and cabinets while Melissa cleaned every touch surface with disposable wipes. The wipes, along with any remaining trash and food packaging, was loaded into a plastic bag and carried out. Melissa's last act was to wipe the outside doorknob. By the time the first streaks of light appeared in the east, they were on the road.

A fair number of vehicles were already out, those of laborers and businessmen making an early commute to beat the traffic. The Nissan glided along anonymously within their midst, the tinted windows hiding Todd and Melissa in their colorful beach wear. Melissa had done a bang-up job purchasing the necessaries: sunglasses, Hawaiian shirt for Todd, sandals and straw hat for herself. To any observer, they appeared to be the very model of the foolish European tourist couple.

They took an off-ramp, leaving the thickening traffic behind and exiting the city proper to head toward the coast. At this hour, there was almost nobody on the road. Nevertheless, traffic cones had been set up, narrowing the multiple lanes down to a single one. Barriers and flashing lights appeared in the road ahead.

"Checkpoint ahead," Todd said.

"The bloody cheek of these people!" Melissa shook her head. "When all we want to do is go for a swim."

That state security would have ordered roadblocks to check on people leaving the city was no surprise. Hong Kong had been gripped by spy fever. Todd prayed that their false paperwork would hold up under scrutiny.

A figure appeared in the road ahead—a fat, bored-looking young policeman. He wagged his glowing yellow baton, waving the Nissan to a stop. Todd slowed. The cop's mouth widened in a yawn as he sauntered toward the driver's side window. Todd rolled it down, pasting a goofy smile on his face.

The Chinese cop crouched and peered into the car, taking in their ridiculous wardrobe and rear seat piled with lawn chairs and inflatable beach toys. He snorted, the edges of his lips curling in amusement.

"Uh...*papiers?* Papers? *Papieren?*" He knew enough to make several language stabs in European tongues.

Todd handed over the falsified rental paperwork and the tourist pass. The cop seemed on the point of pressing them for their passports, but then checked his watch.

Probably nearing the end of his shift, Todd thought, remembering the yawn.

In the end, the cop shrugged, opting against pressing the matter. He examined the paperwork, compared the names, took another look inside the car, and handed the documents back across.

Then he waved them on.

———

Within a short time, they topped a rise and were staring down at an ocean glittering in the early light.

"Lovely," Melissa said. "Care to let me in on the plan, Dickie?"

"It's unconventional."

"It bloody well better be!" She shook her head. "At this point, there's no going back. I'm sure that young cop will be in hot water when he reports letting us through. I'm surprised we haven't been tailed."

"So far, so good." Todd checked the stretch of highway visible in the rear-view mirror. It was still blessedly empty. "The clock will start ticking once we appear at the resort. With no reservation, we'll definitely pique the interest of the management and whatever security personnel they have on staff. If we move in slowly and blend in, we can expect a delay before any real action is taken. But not a long one."

He took the off-ramp and began descending toward the walled resort. With its rolling lawns and generous, wide open spaces, it couldn't be a greater contrast to the city if it tried. The Nissan coasted onto the property. At this early hour, the staff was barely in evidence. A single gardener dickered with a flower bed by the entrance, but otherwise things were quiet.

"How are we set for cash?" Todd asked.

"I still have some change from the shopping trip."

"That should do for now." Todd found the parking lot and steered into an empty space. The gardener didn't even look up as they stepped out, pausing to grapple their beach gear from the rear seat. "Come on," Todd said, hefting a folding chair under each arm. "This way."

He guided them around the edge of the hotel to a path. The Google street view was thankfully up-to-date: the path wound around the side of the main building to a wide terrace. From there, steps led down to the beach. Todd scanned the waterfront. The sand had been tidied up and raked prior to the day's recreation. A cabana-style bar and grill dominated the middle portion of the tourist area. A tired-looking Chinese woman in an apron was tidying up behind the counter. Close by the water line were some boat houses and beach rental outlets. Todd led them close to the tideline and set up the folding chairs. Then he checked his watch and stared out at the horizon.

"Should be along any time now," he said.

"What should be along anytime now?"

"The HMS *Prince of Wales.*" Todd shrugged. "They just transited the Taiwan Strait."

"The…what? The bloody aircraft carrier? *That's* your plan?"

"Part of it."

"Dickie…"

"How about a coffee?"

She didn't reply. In all fairness, her jaw had dropped and she was standing there stupefied. So, he shrugged and made for the grill counter.

"Hello!" The Chinese woman switched on her customer service smile and her basic English skills. "Up early! Up early!"

"Yes, indeed!" He mimed drinking motions with his hand. "Coffee? Coffee?"

"Ah!" She nodded and poured two cups. Rather than accept Todd's money, she laid a resort chit in front of him. He signed a name and provided a smeared and blurry room number in the blank provided. She filed it away without a second glance. Todd returned to Melissa, noting her expression of disbelief.

"Coffee?" he asked innocently.

CHAPTER FORTY-THREE

HONG KONG—0602 HRS (GMT +8)

"You're a bloody maniac, Todd."

"Yes, but I'm His Majesty's maniac."

Todd sipped his second cup of coffee and watched the beach come to life around them. Early bird tourists appeared in flocks of two, three and more, hauling their beach chairs, sack lunches, broods of children along with them. Hotel waiters waited in the shade of the cabana grill, ready to serve from the tray of pastries and baked goods the woman behind the counter had prepared and laid out for guests. And, to Todd's pleasant surprise, a man in a blue shirt and captain's hat yawned and stretched as he wandered onto the marina launch to attend to opening up.

Todd made out a distant silhouette on the horizon and smiled.

"Jesus, Dickie. Don't look now."

Todd turned.

He clocked the new waiter immediately. Dressed in the same immaculate black pants and shoes, he wore a white smock that was slightly different than those of the others. It had subtle red piping around the sleeve hems and a CCP pin on the lapel. He was leaning across the grill counter, speaking intently to the woman there. As he spoke, she turned and glanced at them hurriedly before averting her gaze and answering the man's questions.

"He'd be a party boss," Todd said. He stood up and stretched in a leisurely fashion. "Time to get moving. Wait here. I'll be right back."

The party boss finished speaking with the girl. With a final glance their way, he hurried back toward the hotel, lifting a cell phone to his ear as he went.

Todd marched down the marina dock to the boat house. The man in the captain's cap was hosing down a pod of Sea-Doo jet skis.

"Hallo!" Todd grinned broadly and gestured toward the jet-skis, holding up two fingers. "Two, please."

The captain's cap looked up doubtfully and said something in Chinese. Todd flashed some cash. The man peered at the watch on his wrist, appraised Todd afresh, and smiled. Todd handed across a few bills, nodded thanks, and wandered back over to Melissa. She regarded him with a fixture of doubt and fascination.

"Right, luv. Time to bid China goodbye."

"Jet skis? Dickie. Really?"

Todd grinned, took hold of her hand, and guided her down the jetty to the dock master. He had just finished hosing off the Sea-Doos and had loosened two from the pod. One was tied to the dock while the other growled, its engine engaged and exhaling its propulsive exhaust into the water behind. The dock master held it with one hand, waiting for Todd to mount.

Todd saw the party boss appear at the top of the hotel steps with a policeman. They began hurrying down toward the beach.

"Ladies first," Todd said, untying the second jet ski. The dock master held the first one steady as Melissa swung a leg over the seat and crouched to take the handlebars.

"Stay inside lagoon," the dock master said, pointing to a buoy. "Not past there."

The cop and the party boss had reached the beach and were scanning around frantically.

"Cheers, mate," Todd said. He boarded the jet ski, hit the start button, and coasted away from the dock just as the cop shouted and waved his arms frantically, jabbing a finger at them.

———

"How you finding it, Melissa?"

"Oh, it's brilliant!" She grinned from beneath the brim of her ludicrous straw boater. Her face was obscured by oversize sunglasses. Her figure straddled the jet ski's fuselage like a walrus in a swimsuit. "It's like my little Triumph back home."

"You ride motorcycles?"

"Bloody right. Doesn't everybody?"

Todd looked back at the resort as they sailed past the safety buoy. It had shrunk considerably, the beach now a ribbon of brown against a large dark mass. But he could nevertheless make out the form of a policeman speaking frantically into a cell phone. They were well beyond resort safety limits and heading for international waters.

The HMS *Prince of Wales,* while closer, was still a dim form in the distance. They had quite a ways to go, but Todd knew the gas tanks of the SeaDoos contained more than enough fuel to get them there. And Sir Reginald had notified the command crew that Todd and Melissa were coming. No doubt the bridge watch was on alert and scanning for them.

Time to send the signal, he thought.

He waved to notify Melissa and then brought his jet ski to a full stop. She buzzed up alongside his and did likewise.

"What's up?" she asked, now apparently quite at ease with the notion of navigating the Pacific aboard a SeaDoo.

"Time to ring the doorbell." Todd drew a dark green cylinder from the waistband of his swim trunks, pointed it at the clouds, and pressed a button on the side. Immediately, an incandescent purple flare climbed skyward to detonate in a blast of purple light. If the ship had been unaware of their presence, that was no longer the case. One purple flare meant they were in-bound. A second one would be loosed if they got into any trouble.

"They'll be waiting for us," Todd said. "You're doing alright?"

"Enjoying the ride, actually." She grinned and gunned her throttle. Todd did likewise and they resumed course for the carrier.

It was a fine and balmy day—perfect for the unconventional mode of transport they had chosen. The sky was mild and forgiving, the seas quite calm. Todd figured another forty minutes would put them in close visual range. So far, the *Prince of Wales* was the only vessel he'd seen. Just in case, he began a full 180-degree scan of the horizon. It wasn't until he was ending the arc of the scan that he saw the thin, lacey wake of the ship approaching from around the edge of the headland. Low in the water and moving fast, the navy patrol boat was on an intercept course.

CHAPTER FORTY-FOUR

HONG KONG—0712 HRS (GMT +8)

"We've got company."

Todd waggled his head in the direction of the approaching patrol boat. Melissa clocked it and asked, "Can we outrun them?"

"No. But we can make it difficult for them." Todd examined the fairway ahead. "Follow me."

He twisted the handlebars, guiding the jet ski off to the left and away from the oncoming patrol boat. The point now was to put as much distance between them as possible. Todd twisted the jet ski's throttle to the limit and Melissa did likewise. But even with them moving as quickly as possible, the patrol boat was continuing to gain on them.

He switched course again, veering them back in the direction of the *Prince of Wales*, Melissa following. The patrol boat was forced to switch course again. But now its presence was plainly visible to the carrier.

"Cutting it close!" Melissa cried above the whine of their motors.

"Things will get dicey!"

The patrol boat loomed off to starboard. Crewmembers were already clustering on the foredeck, two with ropes and a boat hook. The other two held assault rifles.

"Come on!"

Todd twisted the handlebars again and began leading them in a dead run, straight for the side of the carrier. Gunfire rattled behind them, then a voice over the public address system of the navy boat boomed in Chinese, no doubt ordering them to stop for boarding and inspection.

As if! Todd snorted, twisting the throttle to the limit.

The carrier was close enough now to make out details of the hull. Todd could discern the tower and superstructure, the silhouettes of jets on deck and the launch platform lowering. Squinting into the sea spray, Todd thought he could make out black clad figures mustering around a Zodiac. So they were sending reinforcements...

But will they make it in time?

The patrol boat was almost on top of them. A few experimental shots from the riflemen in the prow probed the distance between them. For now, they were too far ahead to reach. But all that was changing by the second.

Once they're on top of us, they'll either shoot or just plough us under.

The Zodiac with the Special Boat Service crew had left the carrier and was speeding toward them. But there was no doubt they would arrive second. The patrol boat was almost on top of them when a thin whine filled the air. Todd looked up.

A Harrier, having launched from the carrier's desk, was inbound, engines shrieking as it assumed a low-altitude approach attack posture, and lined up the weapons bristling beneath its wings on the patrol boat.

Todd smiled as the navy vessel turned and beat a hasty retreat back to shore. Soon the Zodiac came into range and took them onboard.

After a shower and a change of clothes each, Todd and Melissa met in the enlisted man's mess for a meal. Quinn, the executive officer, welcomed them with a smile.

"A rather unconventional mode of travel you chose," he said with a laugh. "I don't think I've ever seen a jet ski used by agents to exfiltrate from foreign territory."

"The SeaDoo is actually a fine machine," Todd said. "Given that the limit for maritime waters is twelve miles and the tank on our jet skis gave us enough to travel ten times that distance, I knew we'd be fine. The reception committee was most welcome."

"Our pleasure." Quinn sipped his coffee. "After our Harrier chased off the patrol boat, the People's Liberation Army Air Force scrambled jets. But it was mostly for show. They kept to their own coastline and didn't bother coming after us. You're safe in British territory now."

"Much obliged."

"We did take delivery of some material of yours." Quinn handed across a locked canvas pouch of the kind used for diplomatic traffic. "Apparently related to your mission in China." He stood. "I'll leave you to it. Good luck."

"Thank you, commander."

They finished breakfast and hurried back to the cabin that had been set aside for their use. Todd keyed his passcode into the digital lock securing the canvas pouch and pulled open the top. Inside was a three-ring binder. He withdrew it, scanned the contents quickly, and handed it across to Melissa.

"We've come down to the final act," he said. "We know where Raptor is. Or, more accurately, where he is headed. GCHQ was able to intercept a phone call."

Melissa's lips moved as she read the fourth page to herself. "Summit meeting. On the campus of George Washington University. That's in America."

"Washington, DC. And where, apparently, Raptor is going to meet Jaxom for the hand-off. He's going to provide correspondence Jaxom can use to blackmail the Chinese into giving him controlling shares in the Zamboro diamond project."

Melissa let out a low whistle. "God, that's tangled."

"Bloody right it is." Todd pointed to a paragraph on page six of the dossier. "See here? The summit's corporate sponsors include Bluebird, LLC. That's one of the CIA's shell companies. They use it to finance black projects. Bluebird accounts are the ones used to pay Raptor."

"So, Jaxom is pulling a double cross. He's betraying both his American bosses and his secret Chinese allies. He's rolling the dice."

"For an estimated two hundred billion or more in diamond reserves." Todd shook his head. Jaxom's move was an audacious one. At every turn, both MI-6 and

CIA had been hoodwinked. Todd's hands fisted as he anticipated getting his hands around Jaxom's throat.

Soon, he told himself. *Soon.*

A knock came on the cabin door. Melissa opened it for a young female ensign who stood at attention. She gave them both a salute before speaking.

"The captain says you're to be ready to board a military transport jet within the hour. I'll be back to collect you."

"Thank you, ensign." Todd stepped forward. "You wouldn't happen to know our destination, would you?"

"No, sir. But I'm told it's the first leg of a journey west."

"Well, you can't go too far wrong with the overall direction." He smiled. He was tired of the Orient and ready to head back home.

CHAPTER FORTY-FIVE

HMS *PRINCE OF WALES*, SOUTH CHINA SEA, IN TRANSIT—0929 HRS (GMT +8)

They were placed aboard an RAF jump jet with barely enough time to stow their bags and fasten their seat belts before the engines screamed and they were off. Todd spent the flight studying the contents of the file in the sealed canvas pouch, turning over the details in his mind.

Fact: Shīzi and his corporation had a controlling interest in the newly-discovered diamond fields of Zamboro. The Chinese government, being aware of all foreign business transactions, had involved itself as the silent controlling partner.

Fact: Arnold Jaxom, CIA hacker extraordinaire, was known to have made several unauthorized trips to Zamboro and to have communicated with Shīzi.

Fact: Shīzi was now dead thanks to a contract killer named Raptor, who now had the data drive.

"Raptor is heading to Washington, DC, for the

summit between the US and China," Sir Reginald had said in his latest e-mail. "Jaxom will be in town at the same time. We believe they are likely to do a switch: cash for the drive. Once Jaxom has the correspondence, he has the Chinese over a barrel. He can dictate his terms at the summit."

"And at negotiations for the diamond mines." Todd shook his head. It was a brilliant—and brilliantly simple—move: use one enemy to cancel out another. Divide and conquer.

If Jaxom pulled this off, he could become wealthy and powerful enough to be beyond the reach of law enforcement for life.

———

"So where is this bloody nonsense summit meeting being held again? Some polytech?"

"No." Todd smirked. "George Washington University campus. They're one of America's oldest accredited post-secondary institutions. Been around since the days of Bonaparte. Exactly the backdrop for the hoped-for 'reset' between China and the west."

"'Reset.'" Melissa shook her head. "What is it with Americans and their constant need to start all over again? Seems a bit codependent, if you ask me."

"Johnny Yank. Always trying to please everyone." Todd chuckled, only half-serious. He liked and admired Americans and had knocked around long enough to see the method to their periodic madness in foreign affairs. For no matter how mad they seemed, there was always a reason and method behind it intended to reach geostrategic goals.

Always.

"So Jaxom is going to meet Raptor, get the data key and then sabotage the negotiations by blackmailing China into signing over its controlling interest in Shīzi's diamond enterprise to him."

"That would seem to be his logical end goal."

"At what point do we inform CIA?" Melissa did her best to appear calm and disinterested in his answer, but there were tell-tale signs—twitching of ears, dilating of pupils—that gave away her apprehension and excitement.

And fear, Todd knew.

"We don't. Until after Jaxom is neutralized."

"We're going to kill him?"

"Oh, yes." Todd smiled coldly. "We will absolutely kill him."

They switched aircraft at the RAF Delhi air station and awakened at RAF Northolt just north of London. There they transferred to a Foreign Ministry Lear Jet, received false IDs and travel papers before being allowed to collapse into the exhaustion that had been plaguing them both since Hong Kong. They had crossed *how* many time zones?

More flight. More narcotizing, encapsulated darkness. Artificial day and night bounded by the raising and lowering of window shades. And a final growl of engines as the British government jet lined up for the final approach to Andrews Air Force Base. Local time was late morning.

They landed and were greeted at the bottom of the stairway by an American state department official who barely even glanced at their passports before waving them through.

"His Majesty's trade and finance? Sure, fellas. No problem. C'mon in."

"I wonder if he even noticed I'm a girl?" Melissa moaned, retrieving her passport and muttering at Todd.

"You are the very model of a modern major general," Todd reassured her.

Their State Department pal was even kind enough to call a taxi for them. They waited by the curb in a light rain as a pair of headlights rounded the distant curve of the on ramp. Soon they would be in the thick of DC traffic and on their way to the university campus. With each second during which they were as exposed as they now were ticked away, he felt a major sense of dread that gave way to impending relief when the cab pulled up beside them.

"George Washington University campus, please," Todd said.

"You won't want to go there," the cabbie said. "Place is completely blocked off. Crawling with security prior to the summit."

"That's why we're here," Todd said.

"No kidding?" The driver, an expression of marginal surprise crossing his face, turned and steered toward the campus. "You guys security?"

"No. We're translators with the trade commission," Melissa lied. "There are over two hundred translators that have been hired for the talks."

"You speak Chinese? Cool!"

They floated through the city toward the GW campus. Todd noted the thickening presence of police and fire vehicles as they approached the main gate.

First responders and emergency services were staging up prior to the main event.

"You can let us out there," Todd pointed to a newspaper stand. "We're meeting our team there."

The driver let them off, wishing them luck as he cruised away. Todd and Melissa lingered on the sidewalk for a long moment, examining the crowd of police and government personnel surrounding the campus. Finding their way in—let alone finding a lone man who was a master of disguise and an expert at sneaking in and out of places—would be difficult enough.

"We have to figure out a plan," she said.

"We have to figure out surveillance," he said.

She shook her head. "Needle in a haystack."

"At the very least."

CHAPTER FORTY-SIX

The arrival of the Chinese president was greeted with much media fanfare. It seemed every television within sight of their hotel was tuned to the live feed from Andrews. It was the first state visit by a sitting Chinese president in over a decade.

In keeping with the "off-the-books" nature of their mission, Todd and Melissa were staging up as if they had to make do without embassy support. This was not exactly the case. They had the support of the embassy intelligence personnel but opted to minimize it. Communications and equipment needs were being met via dead drops at a local storage facility. And although they were in an allied country, they opted for the added security of TidalRip to cover their digital tracks.

So, they monitored President Sheng's arrival via their hotel room TV. Todd sat in the desk chair drinking a cup of coffee while Melissa watched from the edge of the bed, nervously unwrapping a lollypop. Laptops and cell phones littered every available surface of the room from their efforts to furnish an informal intel/comms hub with sufficient coverage. Onscreen, the limos were en route from the airport.

"Sheng's under a lot of pressure at home," Todd noted. "His ascension to the senior party ranks was not without opposition. His tenure looks precarious."

"Could be," agreed Melissa. "I'm no China hand, but I read the papers. Plenty of infighting in the Central Committee. If Raptor is looking for an opportune moment to tip the apple cart, he's found it. Sheng's delegation will be walking on eggshells just now."

They watched as the Chinese president's motorcade wound through the city, observed from on high by news helicopters. There were a dozen network and freelance pilots circling over the university campus and metro downtown area just now, providing them with ongoing video feeds of traffic. At least two of the cell phones were tuned to chopper feeds.

"...and we can see the president's motorcade turning onto the main avenue."

The news anchor narrated as images from the air filled the screen.

"The gates to the campus are just a few blocks away and— oh. Okay, we have some disruption—the motorcade has been waved to a stop by DC police..."

"Looks like protestors," Melissa said. "Bunch of kids sitting down in the street to block traffic."

Todd laughed. Although he had been personally inconvenienced by climate activists blocking roads in

London, he found it rich that the president of China had to cope with such indignities.

"I doubt it will last long," he said. And he turned out to be right. As they watched, a van pulled up and disgorged a dozen policemen, who immediately began dragging protestors off the road.

"We should all get that kind of service," Melissa complained, popping the lollypop into her mouth.

"Well, become a head of state and you'll get all the police intervention you want," Todd joked. He stood and checked his watch. "Time for a drop. I'll be back soon."

———

Even though America was an ally, the intelligence staff at the British embassy was conscious that even allied intelligence services kept an eye on their declared agents in-country. Among the vehicles in the embassy motor pool was a panel truck painted up to resemble vans used by a local courier company. The vehicle had proven their lifeline to needed information and equipment.

Todd waited at a table in a fast-food restaurant beside a tall office building at which the courier truck made regular stops. Todd finished his coffee and stood as the truck rounded the corner and pulled up at the office building. He waited until the driver rose and went indoors to go and stand on the corner, feigning a wait for a cab. Todd greeted the driver as he emerged from the lobby and followed him through the door and into the rear of the vehicle.

"Got a package for you here," said the man, handing

over a wrapped parcel about the size of a shoe box. "Anything for our team at the embassy?"

"No." Todd shook the box experimentally, hearing the shift of equipment inside. "Nothing from us. Just noting this morning's motorcade."

"Us, too," grunted the driver. "CIA is all over it. They've got teams posted up and down the roadway and all over the university campus."

"No surprise there," sighed Todd. "Thanks for the update."

"No problem."

———

Melissa confirmed the driver's news upon his return to the room.

"I've managed to pull together the various media and internet live feeds around George Washington," she said, tapping her laptop. A multi-pane window was open revealing various shots of the campus. "The Americans have gone all-out on security. They've got the local cops, elements of their national guard...plus Secret Service and CIA. They're all focused on the conference center."

Todd studied the image of the largest building. Both US and Chinese flags were flying outside its entrance, and the sidewalk and walkways before the main door were crowded with uniformed police.

"Snipers on the rooftops, too," Melissa noted.

"And there will be security in helicopters overhead." Todd sighed and shook his head. "Getting in and out of there undetected is going to take some doing."

"We need a way to pass on and off campus without arousing suspicion." Melissa frowned. "Any ideas?"

Todd smirked. "I can think of one."

———

Like most universities, George Washington was hemmed in by restaurants and bars. Todd and Melissa took a walk to the busiest of these—a bar and grill that was part of a large national chain. They sat at a table near the bar and monitored the comings and goings of students. At one point, a group of about a dozen crowded around the bar. Todd tuned into their conversation sufficiently to learn they had gathered to wish a friend of theirs farewell as his graduate studies would have him moving abroad.

"That's the one," Todd said, nodding toward the tall blond kid who was the recipient of all the attention. "Excuse me."

Melissa watched as Todd made his way to the washroom, pretending to be slightly drunk. He bumped into the tall student and apologized. When he returned from the washroom, he had the kid's wallet in hand.

"Okay," he told Melissa quietly. "Time to leave."

CHAPTER FORTY-SEVEN

Later that night, Todd changed into slacks and a pullover, heaved a backpack full of books over one shoulder, and left the hotel. He stole an unchained bike from a rack outside a coffee shop and pedaled toward the George Washington campus. Traffic was still heavy at this hour but once he turned off the main thoroughfare and angled toward the east gate, the streets emptied. Two DC policemen and a man in a dark suit with an earpiece and a data tablet stood monitoring the entrance.

"Hi." Todd coasted up with a breezy smile and produced the student ID from the wallet he had lifted earlier. "Adam Carpenter. I'm a grad student here. Just need to get to my office in the economics building."

A policeman accepted the ID and passed it to the man with the data tablet. The physical ID itself had been modified to feature Todd's photo. The man with the tablet keyed in the student ID number and studied the result of the GW student database, which had been hacked earlier that evening by GCHQ to replace Carpenter's photo with Todd's own.

"This checks out." The man in the suit studied Todd. "I need to see another piece of picture ID. Got a driver's license?"

"No." Todd grinned and thumped the bicycle's handlebars. "I don't drive. As you can see. But I...think I have my state ID back at my apartment. I can go get it. No problem."

Two cars pulled up behind Todd. One honked its horn.

The man in the suit exchanged glances with one of the policemen, who shrugged.

"No, that's alright." The man in the suit handed back the ID card. "Keep to the main pathways. Go directly to your destination and return ASAP."

"Will do!" Todd accepted the card back. "Big doings here, huh?"

"Indeed." The man in the suit gave a cold smile and waved him through.

Todd bicycled onto the campus. A few hundred yards inside the gate, he heard a car start behind him. When he glanced back, he saw headlights following him.

He drew a deep breath, bent forward, and leaned into his pedaling. He gained some distance on the car and took the opportunity to bounce up the curb onto the sidewalk. A tree-lined path led to the central buildings of campus. He took it, veering between the trees and into this partially wooded sector of the university. He saw the headlights slow behind him. Playing a hunch, he pulled off the path before a low stone wall enclosing the wooded area and crouched, waiting.

A minute later, the car appeared on the other side of the wall, bare meters from Todd. Anticipating his emergence from the copse, it slowed and he could pick out the features of the man behind the wheel.

Chinese. Dark suit. Working surveillance, he thought. *Chinese security.*

Ordinarily, security for state visits was handled by the security services of the host nation. Todd guessed that there had likely been some dickering between the American and Chinese governments over this that had led to an uncomfortable compromise: the Americans would guard the exterior of the venues while the Chinese would be given free rein to patrol within. That being the case, he doubted there was much open communication between these two rival services.

The car lingered for about a minute, then pulled off in search of him. When it had swung the corner out of sight, he emerged walking the bicycle across the street to the first of the nearest large buildings. A lone DC policeman monitored the entrance. Todd smiled, flashed his student card, and was waved through without so much as a glance. He left his bike by the door.

The building was labeled HUMANITIES. Todd crossed the lobby to the stairwell and took the stairs two at a time to the fifth floor. Emerging into a dimly lit hallway, he walked until he found some windows that looked out onto the grounds.

There. Not far from where he stood, a cluster of police vehicles was parked around the convention center, blue and red strobe lights pulsing. Todd removed a pair of night-vision binoculars from his backpack and focused them on the area, which was thick with cops and security personnel. Black-suited Secret Service agents mixed with the law enforcement teams, some of who guided dogs around the perimeter. The place was sewn up tight. The binoculars came with a data port that allowed him to take photographs using his cell phone camera. He snapped a dozen before the sound of the elevator intruded from down the hall.

Todd took a half-dozen quick steps and retreated into the stairwell. Opening the door a half-inch, he set his eye to the crack and watched.

He recognized one of the Chinese security agents from the car that had followed him. *They must be conducting a sweep of the buildings,* he thought. The man went down the hall, testing doors as he went. While the man's back was turned, Todd closed the fire door and shrunk back against the wall.

A moment later, it opened with a loud *bang* and the security man poked his head out onto the landing. He scanned to the left and the right. Todd held his breath, expecting him to step out onto the landing to check behind the door. But after a few seconds passed, the fire door closed and the man's footsteps receded down the hallway.

Todd took the stairs to the first floor on the balls of his feet. Reaching the ground floor, he let himself out, mounted his bicycle and pedaled back toward town.

CHAPTER FORTY-EIGHT

WASHINGTON, DC – 2130 HRS (GMT -4)

Todd's cell phone chimed a block from the hotel. Following his gut instinct, he pulled over to the side of the road and checked the message. It was Melissa.

> Avoid the lobby. Come to the east
> side of the building. —M.

Todd raised his eyebrows. This was unexpected. He propped the bike up against a mailbox and took a circuitous route back to the hotel, keeping to the shadows along the edge of the sidewalk. When he came to the broad, curving driveway that led to the lobby entrance, he stepped onto the lawn edging the property and made his way through the trees and decorative plants to the eastern wall of the hotel. It was a concrete slab inset with tiny windows like the one in their washroom. Todd guessed this was where the main plumbing works ran up into the structure from under the street. As he approached, the fire door on the ground floor opened and Melissa stood there, looking left and right and pulling the door shut behind him the moment he entered.

"We have a watcher," she said breathlessly. "Got a knock on the door about fifteen minutes ago. Someone from the U.S. State Department here to check our paperwork. They've posted up in the lobby."

"Waiting for me?" Todd followed her up the stairs.

"I rather think so." Melissa paused on a landing. "I told them you were out running an errand."

"Fair enough." They reached their floor and turned toward their room. "What's he look like?"

"Dark suit. Red hair and short beard." She unlocked the door and went to the desk where their forged diplomatic paperwork lay. She handed his across. "Best pop down and say hello."

"Sure thing." Todd pulled off his black sweater and threw a blazer on over his white shirt before taking the paperwork and boarding the elevator to the lobby.

So, the State Department is checking up on us, he thought. *I wonder if that's routine?*

He spotted the man right away. His hair and beard were a bright shade of red and he sat positioned such that he could monitor the front entrance.

"Hallo!" Todd said cheerfully, walking up and surprising the man from behind. "I think you're looking for me?"

The man's startlement was a tremor that flickered across his face and vanished. He composed himself and stood, dragging a wallet from his inside jacket pocket and flashing a badge.

"I'm Nelson. With State Department Diplomatic Security Services." He replaced his badge and accepted the papers Todd handed. "We're just touching base with visiting diplomats and government representatives. Security prior to the summit meeting, you understand."

"Sure thing."

"Where were you?"

It was an investigator's question: short, sharp, and unexpected. He watched Todd as he asked it, scanning for facial tics or other signs of deception. The hawkish gaze disappeared under Todd's answering laughter.

"Went looking for the embassy and got lost," he said with a rueful shake of his head. "Thought I could make it on foot. In the future, I'll rely on taxis."

Nelson absorbed this, allowing his gaze to linger a moment or two longer.

"There anything else?" Todd added in a helpful tone.

"Guess not." Nelson folded and handed back the document. "You have a good evening, sir."

———

The net was being drawn around them in an uncomfortably tight fashion.

"So we've got the Secret Service and the State Department spooks crawling all over every security nook and cranny," he said. "And Chinese state security has a presence on the George Washington campus. I got shadowed by them on my recce."

"Wonderful!" Melissa rubbed the back of her neck as she studied the photos Todd had taken displayed on her laptop screen. "So, we're under scrutiny and our movements are limited. It's almost worse than having an open diplomatic minder."

"Things were much easier back in the old days," he agreed.

"There's no way we're getting anywhere near the convention center without a Secret Service pass," she said. "And even if we do, the chances are the Chinese will start tailing us anyway."

"Alright, then." Todd sighed and sat back, crossing his arms. "So we'll turn it back on them. Do the unexpected. Heighten our profile so we can pick out their minders."

"Just pretend we're ordinary trade representatives going about our business. Nothing to see here…"

"We can start right away," Todd said, standing. "Let's go downstairs to the bar and have a drink."

———

Just two ordinary trade representatives having a nightcap after the day's work. That's the part they played riding the elevator down to the lobby and crossing to the cocktail lounge. Per agreement, each scanned a quadrant within their own view for likely surveillance personnel. The signal they had agreed upon for spotting one was a cough. They made it through the lounge door to a secluded table without either one giving the signal.

"So far so good," muttered Todd. A waitress drifted over and they gave their orders. Melissa ordered a banana daiquiri. Todd opted for a beer.

"We have to come up with a way to get in and out of the hotel unobserved," Melissa whispered.

"Not to mention on and off campus." Todd shook his head. The problems on this mission were multiplying exponentially. "We'll need to reach out to

GCHQ and Six. We may have to change cover and move hotels."

"Might be the most sensible course of action. Go completely underground."

"That might be safest," Todd said. He did not relish posting up in some secret location, possibly stealth camping in a drainpipe as he had done under similar circumstances. But the requirements of the mission came first.

"It's just been one bloody thing after another on this job," Melissa sighed, taking a sip of her drink. "We're due for a little—"

She trailed off, eyes flicking to the lounge entrance.

"Todd," she said, her voice tight. "Don't turn around."

"What is it?"

"Arnold Jaxom just walked in."

CHAPTER FORTY-NINE

Todd remained cool, didn't turn, and focused on slowly and deliberately taking a sip of his drink. Melissa had clocked Jaxom with a swiftness and ferocity that suggested absolute certainty.

"I'm going to hit the bathroom," Todd said as he rose.

"Table by the dance floor. Red bow tie and glasses," she muttered.

Todd turned and began navigating toward the men's room. The glance he flicked at Jaxom's table was innocent enough. But he clocked and catalogued all three faces there, turning away to hide his shock. He let himself into the men's room, stepped into a stall and took a seat, locking the door behind him with a sense of relief.

At the table had been three men, but two of the faces he recognized. Jaxom had been easy to pick out. With his thick-framed glasses and ridiculous blood-red bow tie, he looked like a refugee from the 1950s. But the other two men had been what compelled Todd's attention. One was the Chinese agent he had seen in the Humanities building. The other was the serious black face of David White, CIA's senior deputy director of African operations.

So it comes full circle, Todd thought. A data drive stolen in Africa and brought to China, recovered by a contract killer and brought to DC as a gift to the man planning to make billions by shorting China's plans to enter the world diamond market. *And David White is in league with Jaxom.* CIA was facing major internal subversion at the executive level.

This had gotten completely out of hand. It was time to inform London.

Todd stood and flushed the john, although he had not used it, and let himself out. The Chinese agent entered the washroom. Todd smiled at him as he passed.

"David White?"

Sir Reginald Bull's incredulity was palpable across the video link. Todd sat and waited for the MI-6 lawyer to collect himself. He understood the bafflement completely. David White was an aristocrat in American intelligence circles. To learn that he was involved in subversion would be like hearing the Prince of Wales was secretly a communist and planning to paint Buckingham Palace red.

"There's no doubt about it, Sir Reginald. I saw him in the company of Jaxom and a member of the Chinese security services. A secret meet—quiet, discreet, and 'public' enough to provide deniability in the event it was observed. But the likelihood of that is small. And there's no question, given events, that he's connected to Jaxom's power play against the Chinese."

"Or Jaxom's silent partner in his intended diamond coup." Sir Reginald shook his head. "I'll bring it to the PM, but the play may very well end up being to watch and wait. And those are my instructions to you in the short term. Hold off on any planned action for now until the PM makes a decision. We most definitely *don't* wish to become embroiled in an internal civil war in the CIA. Or, worse, a war between the CIA and the White House. So, keep your head down and your nose clean. Just observe and report for now. Understood?"

"Understood, Sir Reginald."

"I'll get back to you poste-haste." With that, Sir Reginald cut the connection.

———

"We need to find out which room Jaxom is staying in."

"Yes," agreed Melissa. "We do. And if we could get a Falconet inside it, so much the better."

"My thoughts exactly." Todd paused. "Any ideas?"

"Leave it to me, luv," she said. And something in her answering smile was a bit unsettling.

———

What the hell is she up to?

Todd stood nervously in the lobby. Melissa had been in the lounge for twenty minutes, now. When she finally appeared, it was with a glass of white wine in her hands. She paused in the lounge doorway, drained half the glass, and splashed the other half on the sleeve of her jacket. Then she burped, set the glass down on the table, and wobbled through the door in the direction of the reception desk.

Todd grinned and watched with anticipation.

Melissa stumbled to the edge of the reception counter, caught herself, and gazed blearily at the young man working there all by himself.

"Where are my plane tickets?" she demanded.

The young man looked up and blinked. "I'm sorry, ma'am. Your *what*?"

"MY PLANE TICKETS!" She slammed her fist on the counter. "I've been waiting in this damned airport all evening!"

"Uh, ma'am… You're not actually—"

"DON'T TELL ME I'M NOT AT THE AIRPORT!" She hit the desk again. "That's what people keep telling me and it's gaslighting! Gaslighting is a form of abuse!"

"But ma'am—"

"I WANT TO SPEAK TO YOUR SUPERVISOR!"

"Well, it's late and I'm here alone."

"WHAT?"

"He's not here, ma'am."

"BULLSHIT!" She jabbed a finger at the open doorway behind him. "I bet he's back there in that office, hiding from me!"

"No, actually he's in Maryland on vacation."

And Melissa, rather than argue, merely stepped behind the desk, brushed past the young man, and stormed through the door into the office. Once there, she began overturning chairs, knocking over items on desks, and kicking anything and everything out of her way. Not surprisingly, the young man went in after her.

Todd stepped behind the desk, approached the computer, and called up the guest registry.

My God, it's still DOS-based software, he thought.

He heard the crash of breaking glass behind him. Melissa was tearing pictures off the walls.

There! Todd found Jaxom and clicked on the name. A room number came up: 421. He stepped out from behind the desk just as the young man lunged out of the office doorway and made a grab for the phone. Todd saw him dial three digits: 9—1—1.

Melissa emerged from inside the office and sprinted across the lobby with surprising speed to disappear through the front door and down the street.

CHAPTER FIFTY

WASHINGTON, DC—2308 HRS (GMT -4)

Todd was waiting at the bottom of the steps by the east fire door when she crept back an hour later.

"Well done," he said, pulling the door shut behind her. "I must say, you're a very convincing drunk crazy lady."

"I was channeling my Aunt Deirdre." She panted slightly as she climbed the steps behind him to their floor. "She's the terror of Glasgow after you get a few drinks into her. Did you get the room number?"

"Four twenty-one."

"Brilliant! We may have cracked the nut. Raptor may well come here to do the swap."

"My thoughts exactly." He checked his watch. "They were still in the bar as of fifteen minutes ago. Probably still there."

"We'll have to arrange surveillance. Place some Falconets."

"Already done." He smiled. "Put two by his room

door. We'll download the feed when we get back to the room."

"I'll have to keep a low profile after that show I put on."

"The boy only works the night desk. There were no other witnesses."

"CCTV?"

"It, uh, had a bit of an accident." He shrugged. "Sudden inexplicable malfunction that erased several hours of footage. Terrible shame, really."

"Well, accidents *do* happen."

They reconvened around Melissa's laptop. A quick review of the Falconet footage revealed that no one had gone in or out of Jaxom's room.

"I used the Ajax worm to tap their CCTV network," he said. "You can toggle over to a live feed."

She did. A security camera in the lobby could pick out a partial shot of their table in the bar. The back of David White's chair and part of one leg were visible.

"Still there." Todd sat back and rubbed his face. "Okay. What do we have on Raptor?"

"Not much." Melissa sat back and closed the laptop. "I understand Six's file on him is one of the shortest in the entire database. I'm sure you've read it."

He had. The work of the freelance assassin known as Raptor was a blight on the record of every major Western intelligence service. The man had operated with impunity on both sides of the political divide for a decade and a half. He had killed American special forces for the Chinese. He had assassinated Third World dictators for the CIA. He had eliminated Chechen nationalists for Russia. Each time, he had asked for and received exorbitant fees. But he always got the job done and left no trace.

"I have read the file. Because he's so adept at concealing his identity, the only way to identify his signature is by the methodology. And the weapon he uses." Todd narrowed his eyes and sat forward. "Raptor's signature weapon is a Norinco Model 213 chambered with 7.62 rounds. That's basically a Chinese knock-off of a Tokarev. It's a crude weapon but he uses it with great finesse. Always gets in close and uses a silencer. Always gets away without leaving a trace."

"Well!" She hoisted her eyebrows and smirked. "The man obviously loves his work."

———

Sir Reginald got back to him a few minutes before midnight, DC time. It was morning in the UK. Sir Reginald had obviously enjoyed a sound night's sleep. He was dressed and groomed for a day at work as he sat at his desk in Six's Vauxhall Road headquarters.

"Big news first, Sir Reginald. We've found Jaxom. He's here in our hotel. We've installed cameras and have begun surveillance."

"Excellent!" The attorney beamed a rare smile. "It's a cheerful bit of news compared to what I got last night at Number Ten. Went in with the Chief to brief the PM. He was quite clear on how we are to proceed. The first thing is that David White is completely off the table. Consider him untouchable. We are in no way to involve ourselves in the internal affairs of Langley. That's direct from the boss."

"Got it."

"Relations between the two services are at their lowest point in years. Must take care to preserve the 'special relationship.' Now, another thing. Regarding Raptor…"

"We expect he'll rendezvous with Jaxom sometime soon."

"I want you on it. If you come across Raptor, your instructions are to eliminate him. No ifs, ands, or buts. In fact, the Chief would like you to make a special effort in that regard. Would love to hand Raptor's head to the CIA as a trophy. Would do wonders to re-establish good relations."

"So it would." Todd paused. "The Chinese intelligence presence here is very strong. I'm thinking half of President Sheng's entourage is probably some sort of agent. They're all over the campus. The ecosystem here is becoming rather tightly packed."

Sir Reginald thought for a minute. "Any documentation of the presence of undeclared Chinese agents would please the Chief. In amongst all your other priorities…"

"We'll fit it in, Sir Reginald."

"When does the summit begin?"

Todd checked his watch. "In nine hours."

———

Todd treated himself to a room service beer and lay down on his bed to watch TV while Melissa snoozed on hers. Taking up the remote, he activated the flat-screen TV and watched the late network news broadcast. The last members of the Chinese delegation were trickling in. The on-scene reporter characterized them in the voiceover as a group of secretaries, translators, and bureaucrats. But Todd spotted more than a few square-shouldered types in dark suits and sunglasses—a look that had become distressingly familiar.

The film footage ran for a few more seconds after the voiceover. Todd watch the tight gaggle of delegation members proceed down the airline concourse. And then he saw something that struck him as being out of place. So he switched off the TV and used the laptop to find the network's website. Sure enough, that night's episode of the news was available for viewing. Todd called up the video and scanned through it to the film of the delegation proceeding down the concourse.

There.

It was just a flicker-of-a-second blur—the sort of thing one could easily miss. But the more he ran the sequence, the more he became convinced that what he saw was no mirage.

At one point, as the delegation passed, the men's room door had opened and a figure from within stepped out and merged into the crowd.

Raptor was in town.

CHAPTER FIFTY-ONE

WASHINGTON, DC—0607 HRS (GMT -4)

"The *Chinese* delegation?"

"Yes, Melissa."

"So you're thinking Raptor might be…?"

"How else can he hope to blend in?"

"So, he's—"

"I'm fairly sure."

"Cor! *Raptor's a bloody Chinaman!*"

Todd smiled. "Don't say that too loud or else they're apt to consider you some sort of racist."

They would need help.

Todd had a quick video conference with Six. And eight hours later they were driving to the airport to collect their new team member. When they arrived, he was waiting outside the arrivals terminal.

Jimmy Wong, MI-6's top China hand, had the

bleary, rumpled appearance of an overworked elementary school teacher but appearances could be deceiving. He had bags below his eyes, wore a rumpled shirt and polyester tie, and stood in the rain with the stooped patience of a whipped dog as Todd pulled up.

"Jimmy!" He waved and the Chinese agent grinned, slipping in through the unlocked back door. Todd, who had worked with Jimmy on a case involving an exfil from North Korea just a year before, was glad to see him. "Jimmy, allow me to introduce—"

"We've met," said Melissa with a grin. "Last month in Burma."

"The lovely lady has a good memory," Jimmy replied.

"Oh, my," said Melissa, actually blushing.

Todd thanked his lucky stars Jimmy had been available. The man was a tactical genius with a gift for improvisation. He had been plugged, by Six, into so many missions where a Chinese presence would make a difference that he was sometimes called 'Jimmy Fix-It' around the senior officers' mess. In any mission that involved a need for subtlety, Jimmy was the go-to.

They made good time back to the hotel. Melissa led Wong around to the east side fire door and Todd admitted them. Anything they could do to lessen their CCTV footprint was a step worth taking. They took the stairs to their floor, closed the room door behind them, and collapsed around the coffee table with beers from the wet bar.

"We've got Raptor in our sights," Todd explained. "Trouble is that he's mixed in with the Chinese summit delegation. We need a way in."

"So you want me to go undercover in an enemy political delegation to sniff out the world's deadliest assassin?" Jimmy finished his beer and stood. "Thanks for the beer. I'll be leaving now…" He stepped for the door.

They all laughed. Jimmy diverted course to the wet bar fridge and helped himself to a soda. Then he sat back down and rolled a hand, inviting Todd to brief him.

———

"The best way to infiltrate would actually be as an outsider," said Jimmy Wong. Now in shirtsleeves, he hunched over the desk where he was studying the photos Todd had taken of the entourage.

"Why?" Melissa asked.

"Well, for one thing forging credentials will be easier." Jimmy sat back and loosened his tie. "For another, it's a long-standing tradition among Chinese mainlanders to behave as *yan xian* while abroad. Everyone keeps an eye on everyone. And you receive benefits for reporting on your colleagues. So vigilance among the diplomats will be high. But I could easily slip in as a stateside Chinese reporter."

"Like for a local paper?"

"Yes." Fix-It Jimmy sipped his beer. "There are several that are published out of San Francisco." He paused to think for a moment before continuing. "I can mix in with the crowd at their hotel. It will be lower-level functionaries, you understand. The overspill from the embassy. But I can at least move in and become a known quantity. Maybe let slip a few pro-Beijing comments and grumbles about my decadent new homeland…"

Todd appreciated Jimmy Wong's flair for the subtle flourish. *The man's a bloody artist,* he thought.

"We'll keep you updated on any surveillance news at our end," Melissa promised him. "We've got cameras deployed outside the room of Raptor's contact, and we've hacked into the hotel CCTV net. The moment we have a face, you'll have it."

"You need Raptor found."

"Yes," said Todd. "And the sooner the better."

————

They fell into a routine.

Melissa monitored the hotel and Falconet CCTV, keeping a tight watch on Jaxom. Since his meeting with White and the Chinese official, he had remained holed up in his room, dining on room service. She confidently predicted an appearance by Raptor at any moment.

Todd began trying to puzzle a way into the conference center. It presented a mountain of obstacles to overcome but he was determined. Fragments of a plan were coming together. Some assistance from GCHQ might be necessary.

Jimmy Wong applied himself to the job of casing out the campus and the bars in the Chinese section of town. The diplomatic entourage seemed a circumspect bunch. The way Jimmy told it, they were likely under extra special pressure from their handlers to remain close to the embassy and convention center, even when not working. He reckoned they likely had lunch catered in for them, later confirming this with a photo of a truck labeled Gemini Catering. Jimmy Fix-It saw three separate deliveries float in through the east gate over a two-hour period.

"Somewhere in this mix is Raptor," said Jimmy.

"Agreed." Todd sighed. "Now we wait."

The waiting began.

CHAPTER FIFTY-TWO

WASHINGTON, DC—1507 HRS (GMT -4)

Jimmy made a breakthrough six hours into his surveillance of the delegation.

"We Chinese are creatures of habit," he said with a chuckle, laying down his camera and shoulder bag on the kitchen table then easing the kinks from his back. "And yes, it's true. Members of the delegation have been warned to avoid talk with strangers and stay close to home, whether that's in the embassy or hotel housing. But they have found a place to go for drinks. One apparently approved by their handlers."

"Where is it?" Melissa asked.

"I believe the Americans would call it a 'dive.'" Jimmy Fix-It unfolded a map of the campus and pointed to a building near the edge circled in red ink. "It's called Fred's Place. A real hole-in-the-wall. Pool tables. Juke box. Barely any customers. Perfect for a visiting delegation to go as a group, relax in private, and then return without any unwanted interactions."

"Perfect," said Todd. "I'm guessing they'll flock there tonight after the first day of negotiations." He glanced at the TV. The early evening news was broadcasting footage of the opening ceremonies and news conference. If it were possible, the area around the convention center was even more tightly packed with security than before. Multiple channels and internet news feeds repeated the same footage, suggesting that the press were being carefully limited and held within a special bullpen.

"Jaxom still hasn't left his room," Melissa reported. "No guests yet, either."

Todd nodded. The waiting continued but would soon yield results. He was certain of it.

———

Jaxom ordered dinner via room service. Per instructions, the tray was left outside his door. Ten minutes after the knock, the door opened and Jaxom dragged his tray inside before closing and locking the door behind him.

"He's been completely isolated since he checked in," Melissa said. "Not a single visitor."

"It will happen soon." Todd glanced at his watch. "I'm going to check on Jimmy."

"Right-o."

Todd took the elevator downstairs. The same young man who had been on duty at the desk during Melissa's incursion was back. He broke off from his discussion with a hotel security guard when he saw Todd.

"Excuse me, sir," he said. "But weren't you here the night that lady came in and began screaming at me?"

Todd paused, affected a looked of puzzlement, then

smiled. "Yes, I did see her," he said. "She caused quite a commotion. Are you alright?"

"I'm fine, thanks." The clerk smiled. "Do you know the lady?"

"I'm afraid not." He shrugged. "Just some nut-job. Never seen her before."

He stepped toward the exit. He thought he heard a question fired his way by the clerk but pretended not to hear it. He hit the sidewalk and bent his steps toward Fred's Place.

The bar was a short distance from the hotel. *And it really* is *a dive,* Todd thought as he approached. The place was a concrete bunker with a single steel entrance door that loomed beneath a flashing marquee of tired neon.

The interior of the place was ghastly. Ill-lit, it was a wilderness of concrete floors, booths with chipped tables and scuffed leather seats redolent with the stench of bleach. Two lone figures sat at the bar. Todd joined them.

"You new in town?" The man who spoke sat two seats down. He was a red-faced, thick-set man in a pair of overalls. A dirty yellow hard hat sat on the bar beside him.

"Uh, yeah." Todd gestured for a beer and put a five on the counter. "Just visiting. Passing through."

"You sound British," said Hard Hat, toasting him with a beer. "You guys are always welcome here."

"Yeah," said the second man at the bar, a thin black man in eyeglasses. "We've forgiven you for 1776." He laughed and Hard Hat joined him.

"I bet they're visitors, too," said Todd, nodding toward a large booth at which sat a dozen sober-faced Chinese diplomats in black. He noted Jimmy hovering around the edges of the group, playing journalist.

"They're here for the summit meeting," said Eyeglasses. "It's a big do over on campus."

"The Chicoms," said Hard Hat with a note of disgust in his voice. "Suddenly we're friends with them?" He turned to Todd. "How about you Brits? How do you feel about them?"

"Democracy is the worst government system on Earth," Todd said. "Until you consider all the other alternatives."

This got a laugh from Hard Hat and Eyeglasses. Todd finished his beer. Satisfied Jimmy was making progress, he left the bar and returned to the hotel.

———

"Jaxom didn't eat his entire dinner, poor soul." Melissa toasted Todd with a coffee cup as he entered the hotel room. "You see his tray outside the door, there. He left half his steak."

"Probably isn't hungry."

"Bloody waste of good meat."

Todd sighed and took a seat on the edge of the bed. "No sign of Raptor, I take it?"

"No sign of anyone." Melissa toggled between windows. "He's been all alone in there since he arrived. The maid's been in once. And room service at meal times. And that's it."

Todd's cell phone buzzed. It was a text from Jimmy.

> Met a promising contact. Leaving
> Fred's now.

Todd read it aloud to Melissa.

"That's good news." She put down her coffee to unwrap a candy bar. "He was making progress with the Chinese when you arrived?"

"He seemed to be."

Todd took five minutes and gave her a debrief on his trip to the bar. She was calling up photos of the delegation to see if they could identify faces when both their cell phones chimed simultaneously.

"That's Jimmy!" Todd yanked out his phone. Melissa did likewise. On both their screens, a close-up of an area on a DC street map and a pulsing red exclamation point.

"He's activated his spider alarm!" Melissa was already on her feet and grabbing for her jacket.

"He's in trouble." Todd made for the door. "Let's go!"

CHAPTER FIFTY-THREE

WASHINGTON, DC—2113 HRS (GMT -4)

They raced through the streets, guided by GPS, toward the location of Jimmy's alarm. Connecting agents on mission was accomplished through a networked web of digital signals: invisible to phone and computer networks, spider alarms served to notify fellow agents in the event of trouble. And Jimmy had just activated his.

The streets of DC were starting to quiet down but there was still plenty of traffic. The GPS moved them away from downtown into a seedy neighborhood. Todd had not been in DC for years but remembered this strange quality of the town: mixed in with the money and monuments were some of the poorest neighborhoods in the country, where crime, poverty, and drug abuse ran rampant.

"What a dump," marveled Melissa. "I can't believe the Americans accept their capital city being like this."

"Seems sort of fitting," replied Todd. "The richest of

the rich living cheek-by-jowl with the poorest of the poor. It's a good reminder of how the other half lives."

"There!" Melissa held up her phone screen and pointed. "Round the next corner, two blocks down."

Todd turned the corner. And felt his heart sink as he saw the wash of police lights bathing the area in a fog of blue and red.

"Oh, God…" Melissa's moan escaped through clenched teeth.

Todd pulled over and parked a few hundred yards from the scene. A crowd of policemen were gathered around a cordoned-off section of sidewalk. Curious passers-by were being redirected away from the area sectioned off by police tape. The crime scene was roughly trapezoidal in shape, with yellow tape wrapping balcony railings and street lights to prevent intrusion. As they approached, they saw a draped form lying on a gurney. Blood splotches were visible on the covering sheet and policemen were already setting numbered evidence marking cards down among the spatters and chalk outline of a body on the sidewalk.

Todd approached briskly, ducked under the tape, and went to the gurney.

"Hey!"

One of the cops had turned and was advancing menacingly. Todd ignored him, pulled back the sheet and stared down into the drawn, dead face of Jimmy Wong.

"Get back, sir." The cop put a hand on Todd's arm. "Right now!"

"His name is Jimmy Wong." Todd spoke hollowly.

"Wait. You know him?" The cop withdrew his hand and was studying Todd now.

"Yes. We're both with the British government. Here

for trade talks." Todd extended his falsified diplomatic papers. "Jimmy was a friend."

"Okay." The cop accepted and glanced over the papers briefly. "Wait here please while I get the sergeant."

Melissa followed his lead, ducking under the tape and coming to stand beside him. The sheet was still pulled back, with Jimmy Wong's head exposed.

"See that?" he muttered, tilting his chin toward the temple.

"Single bullet hole. At close range. Probably from a silenced weapon."

"Yes."

The officer returned, dragging his sergeant along behind him. The sergeant, an elderly black man with grey hair and eyeglasses, raised his chin and tilted his head back to question Todd.

"You knew the deceased?"

"Yes." Todd repeated his story and flapped a hand at the patrol officer. "I gave him copies of our diplomatic paperwork."

"How did you know he was here?"

"We didn't," said Melissa. "He left the hotel several hours ago. We got worried and began looking for him."

The sergeant nodded. "Do you know where he was headed? Was he going to visit someone or go to a specific location?"

"Uh, that's why we were worried." Todd accepted the paperwork the cop handed back. "Jimmy was…" He paused, feigning discomfort.

"Jimmy was what?" the sergeant asked.

"I don't know if I…" He threw a helpless glance Melissa's way before finishing. "Jimmy was gay. And he had a taste for…anonymous sex."

"Really? Funny thing is, there's a gay bar about a block from here." The sergeant's eyebrows jumped. He turned to the patrol officer. "Get down there with a picture of our victim. Start asking questions. And let them know what happened. Could be we've got a lunatic killing gay men. Tell them to pass the word among their people and be careful."

"Will do, sarge."

The sergeant asked them a few more perfunctory questions and took their contact information. Then he let them go, promising the department would be in touch with further questions.

With a final glimpse at Jimmy's cold form, they turned and headed back to their car.

"Bloody Raptor," hissed Melissa.

"He's onto us." Todd glanced around at the darkened buildings. "Might even be watching us now."

"Bravo. Now we're on his target list."

"No." Todd smiled coldly. "Now he's on mine."

———

The light was blinking on Melissa's laptop when they returned to the room. Seeing it, she hurriedly set down her purse and moved to the keyboard.

"It's the Falconets outside of Jaxom's room," she said. "We've had a contact.

Todd crouched beside her as she rewound film. The notice flag had been triggered fifteen minutes before. The spool halted at the image of a man in a black suit and sunglasses knocking on the door.

"Oh, God," she whispered.

Onscreen, they saw Jaxom answer the door. The

man in the dark suit entered. Two minutes later, he was leaving, shutting the door behind him.

"The lapel pin." Todd's voice was cold. "It's a Chinese Communist Party pin." He stood. "I'll be right back."

He hurried down the stairs to Jaxom's room. Emerging into the empty corridor, he stepped to the door and used a GCHQ app on his cell phone to access the electronic door lock. Looking left and right to ensure he was not observed, he stepped inside.

Jaxom lay sprawled across the desk, a bullet hole in his left temple. The laptop on which he lay had been well and truly smashed to bits. And, if the data drive had ever been in the room, there was no trace of it now.

Todd left everything exactly as he had found it, turned, and left the room, locking the door behind him.

CHAPTER FIFTY-FOUR

"He's going to kill the Chinese president."

Todd was furious with himself. How could he not have seen it coming? Jaxom had made a deal with the devil, and the devil had betrayed him. With the data drive and access to the Chinese president, Raptor no longer needed the CIA hacker. He had everything he needed. After a few seconds' thought, Melissa caught on.

"It's bloody brilliant, actually," she said quietly. "With one stroke, he can cut the Chinese out of the Zamboro diamond pipeline. If he lays that data drive and the head of the Chinese president—figuratively speaking, of course—on Kasinga's desk, he becomes the godfather."

"All he needs to do is get them to sign Jaxom's assets over to him. And he's got the perfect motivation."

"Which is?"

"Assassins like Raptor usually don't get to retire.

But if he swings a deal with Kasinga's government, Zamboro can become his safe haven. And he'll be arguably the richest man in the country."

Melissa shook her head. "Every man wants to retire to a place he can call his own."

———

If they were going to stop Raptor, they needed a way into the convention center. But getting through the labyrinth of security, Chinese undercover surveillance, police, and Secret Service without the proper passes would prove quite a task.

Todd wracked his brains. Truth be told, the situation was starting to get to him. He was grateful for Melissa's presence. She had a gift for situational improvisation and computers. But she wasn't a tactical thinker. And although he was pleased she left such details to him, he rather wished for another strategist off whom to bounce ideas.

Given how much chocolate she eats, you could bounce almost anything off of her, he thought, and immediately regretted the unkind sentiment. But when he saw her produce another in an endless series of candy bars from her purse, inspiration struck.

———

After a few hours' rest, they were up and parked across the street from their best bet to enter the convention center undetected.

"Now *this* is the kind of undercover job I can really sink my teeth into," she said. Real excitement bubbled in her tone.

"Now, now... No sampling the merchandise, dear." He smiled.

The Gemini Catering Company owned a large windowless building a few miles from downtown. Surrounded by a tall wire fence, the compound boasted a fleet of trucks emblazoned with the company logo. Dawn had broken just the hour before, but already employees were arriving for work—the bakers and cooks who would get to work preparing the day's first meals for delivery to the Chinese embassy and the convention center.

"So." Melissa glanced at him. "What's the play?"

"We're going to wait for the first morning delivery to roll out. Then we're going to seize the truck and whatever event passes the caterers have." He tipped a nod in the direction of the campus. "Then we're going to drive right into the conference center."

Melissa pondered this for a long moment. "Right in the front door, then?"

"Right in. They won't expect us."

"No." She puffed out her cheeks. "I should think not."

They didn't have to wait long. Within an hour of the cooks and bakers arriving, the drivers began tramping out to their vehicles. Two caught his eye in particular— a man and a woman who seemed to be a supervisor headed toward one truck. The woman held a clipboard from which she pulled two laminated passes on lanyards, passing one to the driver.

"That's our truck," he said, pointing.

"Right-o."

As the two boarded one of the delivery vans, Todd switched the car on. When they pulled out of the gate and turned toward campus, he followed them.

———

Traffic was sparse in this part of the city so early in the morning. The van scrupulously followed all traffic laws, which was to the good. It's what Todd was counting on.

Eventually, the van stopped for a red light at a deserted intersection.

"Right." Todd opened his door. "You take the wheel. Follow us."

"Will do," said Melissa, sliding across the seat to the driver's spot.

Todd casually ambled up to the passenger side of the van. Like many such delivery vehicles, this one had an open space where a door would normally be. Todd advanced toward the woman with the clipboard who sat beside the driver.

"Hallo!" he said with a friendly smile. Dragging out his gun, he stepped onboard, forcing the woman out of the passenger seat. "Do as I say and you both live. Understand?"

The woman, a middle-aged type with a florid face and short curly blonde hair, stood dumbstruck with fear. The driver, a youngish fellow with a scraggly beard and a ball cap, put up his hands in terror.

"Whaddya' want me to do, man? Take my money. Take whatever you want!"

"Relax." Todd stepped into the rear of the van, grabbed the woman by a lapel, and hurled her back into the passenger seat as the light turned green. "Drive where I tell you. Straight on now. Normal speed. Nothing funny or I put a bullet in you."

Shaking, the driver edged into the intersection. Todd reached down and grabbed the laminated badge hanging from the woman's neck.

"These. Security passes?"

"Y-yes…" She licked her lips, eyes darting nervously around the cabin.

"For what? The embassy? The convention center?"

"Both!" She held up the badge. Todd recognized the logo of the US Secret Service. "My company won the bid for all the catering at the summit."

"Congratulations!" Todd grinned. "You must be very proud."

"Please don't kill me."

"Only if I absolutely have to," he assured her. Poking the driver, he pointed with the gun. "Turn in here."

CHAPTER FIFTY-FIVE

WASHINGTON, DC—0602 HRS (GMT -4)

The van turned into the indoor parking garage, with Melissa following close behind. Todd directed the driver to take the ramp down to the lower level. In the vast space were only a few cars and no pedestrians. Todd directed them to park the van in a distant corner. Melissa pulled up beside him.

"Alright. Get out." Todd waved the gun.

The driver and supervisor, hands raised, stumbled out of the van. Melissa was waiting beside the rental car.

"Back seat," Todd told them. "Now."

She held open the door as the van driver and super slid into the back. Todd opened the driver side door and leaned in.

"This won't hurt," Todd said, producing the small silver tranquilizer gun. "Not until you wake up anyway, in about eight hours' time. Then you'll have a splitting headache. But at least you'll be alive."

"Who are you?" demanded the supervisor, finally finding her courage.

"Nobody," Todd said, and shot them each with a tranq. They stared with surprise at the flechette's impact, then swooned into unconsciousness. Todd reached in and plucked the lanyards from their necks before arranging their bodies so they were both lying across the back seat. Then he locked the car and handed a badge to Melissa.

"We're on the clock now," he said.

She checked her watch. "We certainly are. Let's go."

————

Todd drove, placing Melissa in the supervisor's role. As they approached the campus, she flipped through the contents of the woman's clipboard.

"There's a vehicle pass here, too," she said, examining a half-sheet marked with the Secret Service logo. She handed it across to Todd as he pulled up at the east gate of campus. Two policemen and a Secret Service agent were waiting.

"Breakfast?" asked the one cop, poking his head in and glancing at the cargo area. It was piled high with meals concealed beneath warming hoods.

"Breakfast it is," Todd said, offering the pass. The cop accepted it and handed it to the Secret Service agent, who consulted his data pad.

"Mind if I have a look?" the cop asked.

"Help yourself!" Todd smiled. The policeman walked around to the back of the van and tugged open the access door. Todd watched in the rear view as he boarded and looked around, pausing to pull the cover off of random meals.

"You guys new?" The Secret Service agent handed the pass back to Todd.

"We're management from the Maryland outlet," Melissa said. "They were short-staffed here so brought us down to help out." She held up her laminated pass. The Secret Service man glanced at it, then at Todd's before nodding and stepping away. The access door at the rear of the van shut.

"It's all clear," said the cop.

"Okay." The Secret Service agent nodded. "You're cleared to enter."

"Thanks," Todd said. And held his sigh of relief until they were on their way.

They floated onto the still campus along the same road Todd had entered by bicycle. He noted the same car that had followed him parked by the side of the road. But the Chinese agents inside merely noted the catering van as it swept by and did not follow.

Todd grinned. *Getting slack there, boys,* he thought.

There was another security gauntlet at the edge of the community center, this one both uniformed and plainclothes Secret Service. A uniformed officer waved the van to a stop while another approached with a leashed canine wearing a secret service dog vest. The man with the canine circled the van while the uniformed officer approached the window. Todd, expecting another shakedown, was surprised when the uniform glanced in, saw their badges, and gave them a thumbs up.

"Nice and easy," whispered Melissa.

"Careful or you'll jinx it."

The canine moved off and a third uniformed officer approached with a mirror on a long pole. He swept it under both sides of the vehicle, checking for suspicious items in the undercarriage. His sweep ended at Todd's window.

"What's for breakfast today?" he asked cheerfully.

"Eggs, toast, and waffles," Todd replied.

"Bring any for us?" The Secret Service man grinned.

"Ha!" Todd returned the smile. "If we have leftovers, I'll let you know."

"Damn right. Service gets dibs before the cops on food, ya' know."

Todd chuckled and steered the van toward the conference center loading dock.

Security was lighter within the cordon, but no less evident. Instead of groups of agents, solitary Secret Service men in suits and dark glasses stood spaced at hundred yard intervals, scanning everything from behind their mirrored shades. One stood alone on the dock, eyeing the van as they approached.

"This is going to be the real test," Todd said. "He's probably been manning the dock for a few days."

"He probably knows the regular delivery crew."

Todd felt a sense of uneasiness rise in his stomach. Although the agent's eyes were covered, something in the set of his jaw and the furrow of his brow suggested he knew something was out of place. He waved the van to a stop.

"Pull out your cellphone and pretend to make a call," Todd said.

Melissa did exactly that as the agent approached the driver's side window. Todd rolled it down and pushed the vehicle authorization and both laminated badges toward the agent.

"Hi," he said. "I know. We're new faces…"

"Where's Carol?" The agent was scanning the dashboard and the rear of the van, ignoring the paperwork Todd proferred.

"Workplace accident," Todd said. "She's in the hospital. We're getting the manager on the phone for you now so you can vet us."

"Okay..." Only now did the agent's attention go to the paperwork. He scanned it quickly, handed it back, and addressed Melissa. "Hang up your phone, miss."

Melissa, a look of surprise on her face, did just that. Then the agent said the words Todd dreaded to hear:

"Step out of the van, please."

CHAPTER FIFTY-SIX

WASHINGTON, DC—0628 HRS (GMT -4)

Todd regulated his breathing, opened the door, and stepped out. Rather than a cooperative smile, he composed his features into something like concern. *I'm just a dutiful and helpful subcontractor who doesn't want to lose the business*, he reminded himself. He modulated his posture and mannerisms to convey submission and cooperation.

The agent beckoned Melissa over to stand beside him.

"Okay," he said. "Ma'am, I want you to go and stand over there." He pointed to the edge of the loading dock then turned to Todd. "I'm going to check the rear of your truck. Open the back for me, please."

Todd complied immediately. Stepping around to the rear of the delivery truck, he gripped the rear door handle and hauled it wide. The agent gestured for him to enter first. Todd did as he was told, careful to keep his face toward the Secret Service man and his hands visible. The look of grim concern still painted his face.

The agent stopped at a rack of food trays, lifted the lid on one, and examined the food items there.

"Is this everything?" he asked.

"We have a small fridge." Todd pointed.

"Open it, then step back. Keeps your hands visible."

Todd bent, pulled open the fridge door wide before stepping back. The agent went to the open refrigerator, bent, and glanced inside. Seeing something not to his liking, he reached in…

Todd calmly drew the silver tranquillizer pistol and fired a dart into the agent's neck. He stiffened and collapsed. Then he stepped out of the truck, closing and locking the doors behind him.

"He's out for the duration," Todd said. "Just a matter of time before they find him. We have to move quickly."

"I'll say." Melissa scanned the loading dock and surrounding area. In the preternatural quiet of the security net, things were peacefully still. "We've still got two and-a-half hours until the next round of meetings begin."

"Raptor will get here early," Todd affirmed. "He'll want to post up and get ready. We're going to find out where."

"Fine." She checked her watch. "We've probably got a half-hour at most before our sleeping agent fails to answer his radio check. Once that happens, they'll search for him."

"And lock down the center once they find him asleep in our truck." Todd sighed. "We'll split up and search the building. Grab your clipboard. I'll carry a few meal trays. Keep up appearances as long as we can."

"This is high-wire stuff, Dickie. I hope you know what you're doing."

"The high-wire is my natural habitat." He grinned. "Let me grab a tray and we'll go."

———

He was tense, back muscles knotted against a bullet as he led the way through the loading dock door to the interior of the conference center. The security presence inside would be massive. Todd knew their chances of success were slim. But they had to try.

And there *was* a massive security presence. But it was not like he expected.

As they entered a long corridor, he saw a lone Secret Service agent engaged in an argument with two Chinese men in dark suits. It was obvious they were with the Chinese delegation, probably listed as translators. But Todd had very little doubt that they were with the Chinese security service.

Todd veered to the other side of the hallway, held his tray aloft and passed by, hearing their bickering as he went.

"—not according to the agreement! *Two* Secret Service agents in main hall…"

"I'm sorry, sir. But we have our orders."

"You must abide by our agreement as regards security operations!"

"Sir, on US soil, the Secret Service has…"

The Secret Service agent glanced at Todd's laminated pass and did not break off his argument. Todd suppressed a grin as he reached the end of the hall.

Too many cooks spoiling the soup, he thought. It appeared that tensions between the domestic security force and diplomatic visitors were erupting in outright clashes. This put the American agents in a very difficult position. *They have to play nice with the fussy foreigners while still doing their job.* He did not envy them this predicament.

He stepped through a doorway into an open area with several corridors branching off to various points in the facility. As Todd stood examining the options, two Secret Service agents hustled by to reinforce their comrade in his dealings with the Chinese delegation.

Safety in numbers, Todd thought.

One of the corridors led to what looked like an indoor parking area. The other, to a room crowded with crates and boxes. Todd chose the third, which appeared to lead into something like a suite of offices. The doors to these were closed and Todd saw no evidence of Secret Service. Likely, those guards had been the ones dispatched to help their beleaguered comrade in the hallway behind him.

When he was partway down the corridor, his cell phone buzzed with a text from Melissa.

> I've found stairs to a top-down
> vantage on the center.

Todd searched for a fire door and eventually found one. The stairs that rose from the landing beyond it rose several floors. Todd took the steps quietly, ears and eyes alert to the presence of agents. He almost bumped into one on the second floor landing but paused when he heard the man's voice speaking into his radio.

"Acknowledged. On my way."

The scuff of the agent's shoe on the landing above

was bracketed by the sound of a fire door clanging shut behind him. Todd guessed he was being called away to deal with another difficult member of the Chinese delegation. Todd made it to the top floor where Melissa was waiting.

"It's a pig's lunch here," she said. "Secret Service and Chinese officials are at each other's throats."

"I noticed," Todd said. He eased the meal tray down onto a nearby table. "That thing's a bloody nuisance to carry around. Show me what you've found."

CHAPTER FIFTY-SEVEN

WASHINGTON, DC—0647 HRS (GMT -4)

Melissa led him to the railing that enclosed the upper level of the conference center. From here, they had a clear view down to the large main room where the talks were being held. Todd could see the rows of tables facing each other, a set of Chinese flags on one and American flags on the other. A group of men in dark suits was flooding into the area from a side door. It seemed that the Chinese delegation had arrived. Early.

"Almost seven," said Melissa, checking her watch. "Talks kick off at nine. My guess is the Chinese president will be here for pre-game in an hour or so."

"And the Chinese are sparing no expense." Todd studied the movements and energy of the growing crowd of dark-suited Chinese. *More hassles for the Secret Service,* he thought. Where had they all come from? Todd guessed they had been tucking away pockets of agents on the campus, perhaps disguised as students? He couldn't see any other way the CCP had managed to get so many people past the security gauntlet and mobilized so swiftly.

"Well, we made it this far," he said. "Somewhere down there is our man. We just need to figure out which one —"

He stopped.

Of course!

It was so blindingly obvious to him now.

"How does Raptor kill?" he asked Melissa.

"Point-blank range," she replied crisply. "A silencer. Shot to the temple."

"Which means he has to get close to his target."

Melissa considered this for a few long seconds before it dawned on her.

"He's part of the Chinese president's security staff!"

"Bingo," said Todd. "And he's bringing in all of these delegates to keep the Secret Service busy and off balance as he prepares to make his move."

"It's bloody brilliant," she seethed.

"We have to get as close as possible to him," Todd said. "Be there when he's staging up to strike. And stop him before he stops the president."

Down below, a group of Secret Service agents appeared. As they waded into the crowd of delegates, they were surrounded by a group of aggressive men who began angrily gesturing and cross-examining them. Todd could tell, even from this distance, that the cool professionalism of the Secret Service was being tested to its limit.

"We would do well to change disguises," he muttered.

"What do you have in mind?"

He told her, and relished her answering look of surprise.

It didn't take them long to find the janitorial room. They floated past clots of Secret Service agents arguing with Chinese delegates and went completely unnoticed in the melee. The room they sought was on the ground floor, not far from the indoor parking area. Todd forced the lock and pushed open the door, closing it behind them as Melissa stepped inside.

"Ah! Here we are." Todd stepped toward a set of orange jumpsuits hanging from hooks on the wall. He pulled one down and held it up. "The absolute latest off the runway in Paris. Nothing but the best for madame."

Melissa wrinkled her nose at the garment. "It smells musty."

"That's the smell of high fashion." Todd pulled down a jumpsuit for himself. Both pulled on their disguises and then turned to the row of janitorial carts lined up by the wall. "We'll each grab a cart. But let's travel in tandem."

"Safety in numbers?"

"Something like that." Todd grasped the handle of one cart and pushed it back and forth experimentally. "The priority is to figure out where the Chinese president's prep room is located."

"Probably close to that indoor parking area." Melissa grasped a cart of her own and pushed. "They have a stage somewhere in here, don't they? If so, then they're likely to have a Green Room."

"Good thinking." Todd pushed open the door an inch and scanned the hallway. It was clear. "Let's get moving."

As they trundled down the hallway in single file, a

trio of Secret Service agents sprinted past, headed for the loading dock.

"They must be worried about their friend," Melissa said.

"They'll be putting out a BOLO for the catering crew." He paused in the middle of the hallway and looked around. "Don't see them anywhere. Do you?"

"Neither hide nor hair."

"Damned caterers," he said, pushing onward. "So bloody unreliable."

———

They entered the garage area. There were no Secret Service agents in evidence but the area was crawling with representatives of the Chinese delegation. The hard men in dark suits and sunglasses barely gave them a glance as they trundled past, pushing their janitorial carts. There were only a few exits out of this area. One was an open archway leading to a carpeted hallway. They entered casually, pushing their carts along boredly like janitors the world over. The corridor reminded Todd of the backstage areas of some theaters he had visited. *Makes sense a convention center would have an area like this*, he thought. As a building dedicated to public spectacle, the conference center would need a place for people to prepare prior to attending their events.

"This is class, Dickie," said Melissa. For effect, she paused and produced a rag and a squeeze bottle of cleaning solution and began wiping doorknobs.

"You're good at that," Todd quipped.

"Bloody right! I had three younger sisters growing up. Lord, they made a bloody mess…"

"Here." Todd paused outside a double doorway. "This looks promising."

He pushed a door wide and stepped in. It was a large, generous room with a conference table, a kitchenette, and separate bathrooms. He pushed his cart inside and began looking around. As he did, a hubbub arose from down the corridor.

"Bloody hell, Dickie!" Melissa stuck her head in the doorway. "The Chinese president's limousine has just arrived!"

CHAPTER FIFTY-EIGHT

WASHINGTON, DC—0708 HRS (GMT -4)

Todd whirled. "Right!" he said. "Get back up to the top floor. Take the elevator. Post up in case I need covering fire on the way out."

"Right." She twirled her janitorial cart and made for the elevators.

Slowly and deliberately, Todd set about cleaning the room. *Every last bloody inch,* he told himself. Like when he was scrubbing the barracks back in the Royal Marines. He gave himself to the task, reminding himself he was playing a role. Playing it poorly would spell his doom.

He heard commotion in the corridor outside. Voices, the sound of footsteps and bodies moving down a carpeted hallway approached; the jarring babble of Chinese arguing and speaking over one another filled the air. *That will be the president and his entourage,* Todd thought. He fought a rising discomfort in his belly and replied himself to dusting the conference table.

Two Chinese minders in dark suits appeared in the doorway. One stepped forward and began to snap at Todd in Chinese but the other held him back with a pat on the arm. This second man moved toward Todd. Tall for a Chinese, slender and stoop-shouldered, he approached with a sad smile.

"Please to finish soon, sir," he said. "Ah, we need the room."

Todd looked up. "Right!" he said cheerfully. "Just done now."

He dropped his rag and spray cleaner into his janitorial cart and wheeled it toward the door. The second guard stopped him on the way out and checked the contents of the cart before letting him through the door.

At the end of the hall, the Chinese president's entourage was mustering around the arriving limousine.

Chinese "diplomats" in dark suits lined the corridor.

Todd pushed his cart across the hall through an open door and began cleaning and dusting a small waiting room area with couches and a coffee table. His shoulders were stuff, muscles tensed against the hand he expected to be laid on him at any moment by a Chinese security agent. But it never came. He was, to all appearances, just a janitor. The assumption was that the janitors, along with the other conference center support staff, had been vetted by security so there was nothing to worry about.

This is just about the best undercover dodge I've ever worked, Todd thought. *Surprised I haven't tried it before.*

His cell phone beeped. A text from Melissa:

> Stand-off in parking area. Chinese
> vs. Secret Service.

Todd typed back:

> Are the Secret Service bringing in
> reinforcements?

She replied:

> If so, no sign of them yet.

Todd went down on his knees to dust the surface of
the coffee table, positioning himself such that he could
see the doorway across the hall. A gaggle of dark-suited
Chinese delegates loitered around the door, some in the
hall, some in the "green room." The tall, stoop-shouldered agent seemed to be in charge. He kept an eye on
things and gave orders, sending everyone hither and
yon with his sad smile.

Todd saw a commotion amongst the agents in the
hallway just as Melissa texted again:

> Chinese president heading your
> way with entourage.

It was game time.

He could hear a large crowd approaching down the
hallway—the Chinese president and his men. Normally,
Secret Service would be present to secure the room and
hallway but the Chinese swarm had effectively
prevented that, forcing the agents to redeploy on the
fly. Outnumbered and forced to restrain their use of
force against foreign diplomats, the Secret Service was
coping, strategizing its next move.

Meanwhile, here was President Sheng of the
People's Republic of China. A small man with round
glasses and a cheerful face, he was a global leader of
unchallenged stature. Todd could see he was accustomed to moving authoritatively, commanding the area
in which he found himself. His men hovered around

him like flies, watching, waiting for orders or signals. He entered the room, followed by a cloud of minders. One of them stuck his head in through the door of the room where Todd worked.

Todd looked up with a blank stare.

The Chinese agent seemed on the point of saying something when the tall, stooped man with the sad smile interposed and said something quietly to him. With a final glance, the man turned back into the hallway.

Sheng was talking now, holding court among the assembled members of his delegation. *Probably giving them a pep talk*, Todd thought. It seemed that making an impression and forcing the Secret Service to redeploy was a power play that Sheng appreciated, even if he hadn't ordered it himself. He was obviously knitting a flag across the hall, talking up the great Chinese presence in global affairs.

Todd had to hand it to him. The man had a flair for the dramatic.

Sheng's informal speech ended to applause. Todd heard a second voice speak in a humble but firm tone. Sheng replied and a number of the delegates filed out of the room. The next thing Todd knew, the tall, stooped delegate with the sad smile was standing in the doorway alongside Sheng. Both watched the delegates approaching the garage area. Todd took out a spray bottle and moved to the opposite wall, out of their line of sight, cocked his head and listened.

The troop of delegates had reached the parking area. Their presence elicited shouts and angry words from the Secret Service agents still trying to resecure the facility.

Another text from Melissa:

Secret Service combat team has
arrived.

Todd knew the Service kept a CAT (Combat
Assault Team) at the ready. Deploying them into the
conference center would allow them to reassert control
over an increasingly ungovernable situation. He poked
his head out the door in time to see Sheng turn and
enter the room, followed by the tall, stoop-shouldered
agent. The doors closed behind them.

They're alone in there.

Todd drew a deep breath, brought out his pistol,
and crossed the hall.

CHAPTER FIFTY-NINE

WASHINGTON, DC—0743 HRS (GMT -4)

He grasped the doorknob and turned but it wouldn't budge. *Locked.* Raptor was being cagey as hell, paranoid right up until the last possible moment.

Todd stepped back, raised a leg, and delivered a massive front kick to the handle and lock assembly. The door blew wide and a shooting pain flared from his ankle to his hip. But he was in.

Things happened very quickly.

President Sheng was sitting at the conference table, eyes on a stack of papers before him. Raptor had turned away, drawn his weapon, and was just preparing to turn back when Todd infiltrated the room. The sound caused the president to look up and see the weapon. He cried out in Chinese.

Raptor, his sad smile and stoop now gone, started, his attention suddenly divided between his target and his attacker.

That's when President Sheng did the unexpected.

Small, bespectacled, unassuming, the Chinese president launched himself from his chair and tackled Raptor. The assassin, taken completely by surprise, was dragged off his feet and brought to the ground. Todd lowered his Browning. With the two tangled up and grappling, there was no clear shot.

He surged forward, pistol raised butt-first to bring down on Raptor skull, when Sheng suddenly screeched and was flung clear of the melee. A wide cut had opened on his forehead.

My God, is he shot? Todd's first panicked thought subsided as he recognized the man had taken a blow from the frame of Raptor's pistol. The assassin rolled free, came up in a crouch, leveled his weapon at Todd, and fired.

The bullet missed Todd's head by bare inches, ploughing a furrow through the flesh of his right shoulder. Just a graze, but it hurt.

Now there were voices and footsteps pounding down the hallway.

Raptor made for the door. Todd spun to go after him. He saw Raptor reach the hallway. He flung his arm out and barked an order at the approaching men. Then, to Barrett's horror, raised his gun and fired on them.

Madness!

The assassin whirled and plunged down the hall toward the fire door.

President Sheng was up, dabbing his bloody forehead with a handkerchief. Trembling and panting, he nevertheless wore a mask of furious resolve.

"Zhuā zhù tā!" he screamed at Todd, pointing at the door. Todd didn't have to understand Chinese to catch his meaning.

Go get him!

Todd plunged through the doorway, making a hard left and pounding down the corridor after Raptor, who had just reached the fire exit and shouldered his way through. The facility fire alarm shrieked. The hallway dimmed to half-light and red lights began twirling through the din and chaos.

Todd followed, stepping out into the back lot of the conference center. There was the loading dock, the catering truck with its doors open and a swarm of Secret Service agents combing over it like ants on a honeycomb. They looked up when Raptor emerged and cried out when Todd appeared, giving chase.

"Stop!" yelled one.

Raptor didn't. He kept sprinting but Todd could see he was starting to favor his right leg a bit. Perhaps Sheng had done him some damage during the brawl. And now Todd was gaining on him. Despite the burning ache in his shoulder, he was gaining on Raptor. He raised his gun…

Raptor chose that moment to stop and turn, raising his own weapon. The combination of their high-speed, the sudden stop, and their mirrored postures caused Todd to plough into the man, the collision knocking both of them off their feet.

The Secret Service were running, too, voices raised, radios and batons deployed as they descended.

Todd and Raptor were a tangle of arms and legs. Todd sought to kick free but Raptor grabbed him. The gun in the assassin's right hand was twisting slowly in his direction. Todd intercepted Raptor's gun-arm with his left.

The Secret Service were barely one hundred yards away.

Todd swung the Browning and smashed the barrel against the Chinese assassin's mouth, bloodying it, knocking loose a few teeth. And then the Secret Service was there, dogpiling on top of them. Todd felt a rough hand on the back of his collar and suddenly he was being dragged free, disarmed, and rolled face down onto the ground by three officers.

"Don't move!" bellowed one, leveling a shotgun at Todd's face. Another came up and clipped handcuffs on him. He was dragged to his feet, hustled along toward the conference center in a bubble of five agents, one of whom held a yelping, snarling canine who twisted on his leash menacingly close to Todd's legs.

A hand grasped his forearm.

"Who are you?" The plainclothes agent pushed his face so close to Todd's that he could see himself mirrored in the lenses of his dark shades.

"I don't quite know how to say this," Todd began.

"Just answer the damn question," snarled the agent.

Todd flashed an innocent smile. "Rule Britannia?"

He was held under guard by six agents in a small windowless room for about half-an-hour. The one in sunglasses returned and read Todd his rights, explaining to him that he was under arrest for violating national security and breaching a Secret Service exclusion zone.

"You endangered the president of the United States, the president of China, and both their delegations," he said. "I hope you have deep pockets and a good lawyer."

There came a knock at the door. One of the guards opened it to admit another agent.

"Sir?" he said. "There's someone here who wants to say something."

The agent in the sunglasses turned.

Suddenly, President Sheng was standing in the doorway with a translator. The Chinese president raised his voice and pointed at Todd, then at the agent in sunglasses, and barked several loud exclamations in Chinese, which his companion translated.

"President Sheng says you must let this man go at once. He says the man interrupted an assassination attempt and saved his life."

The agent in glasses froze. Faced with the completely unexpected, he whirled again on Todd.

"Who *are* you?" he asked again.

"Just a lad from East London." Todd smiled. "God save the King, mate."

CHAPTER SIXTY

WASHINGTON, DC–1103 HRS (GMT -4)

It was a diplomatic train wreck of the first order.

The British Ambassador was called upon to explain the presence of undeclared intelligence agents interfering in a high security event. Having not been briefed, she was unable to do so and later issued an incoherent press statement assuring everyone that her ignorance was, in fact, proof that the "special relationship" remained on solid ground. The embarrassing matter was eventually smoothed over by a chummy phone call between Sir Reginald Bull and the ranking member of the Senate Intelligence Committee, who later briefed the president.

A similar phone call took place between the Chief of MI-6 and his corresponding head of service in Langley. It was a brief call and shortly afterwards, David White was removed from his position as CIA's senior deputy director of African operations. Later that same day, he was removed from his home by armed men in a black van who compelled him to accompany them to a secret location where he would answer an unending series of questions under painful circumstances over the course of several months.

The CIA Director of Operations initiated an internal investigation into the CIA's use of subcontractors. To his management, he reported that the practice of utilizing contract assassins *may* have caused them to inadvertently hire a Chinese national with close ties to the Communist Party. He promised to get to the bottom of the matter, and he did. Raptor's file was located and shredded. He then cheerfully reported up the chain that no such contractor had been found and that Agency operations could resume as normal. For now.

The summit meeting continued, culminating in a dinner where the US and Chinese presidents toasted one another and reaffirmed their commitment to a positive and mutually beneficial trade relationship. Attendees at the dinner described the event as memorable, but that members of the Secret Service seemed unusually nervous. For some reason.

———

Todd was placed in a holding cell in Quantico where he endured several days of being screamed at by various US government functionaries. Investigators from the Secret Service, State Department, CIA, FBI, and DC Police all had a go at him, demanding to know just what the hell he had been doing at the conference center. A sergeant from the US Park Police even came and bellowed at him for a while. Todd answered everyone's questions as politely and coolly as he could but refrained from a full disclosure of his identity and purpose in the country. Fortunately, he was a British and not a Russian agent, so every effort was made to ensure he would be returned undamaged to his country of origin. After all, the "special relationship" had to be taken into consideration.

It was Melissa who finally managed to get in to see him. She had slipped away during the chaos following Todd's arrest and taken refuge at the British embassy, where she had been issued with a cover identity as an immigration attorney. It was these credentials that she flashed once the all-clear had been secured for Todd to confer with counsel.

"Well, Dickie," she said, taking a seat and stripping the cover from a lollypop. "Glad to see you're still with us. How are our American cousins treating you?"

"Oh, well enough." He puffed out his cheeks. "Three meals a day and all the screaming I can possibly want."

"They're hopping mad, Dickie. Everyone is pointing fingers at everyone else. We embarrassed their Secret Service by slipping past them, their State Department by entering the country illegally, and their CIA by out-spying them. If they had their way, they'd hang you and festoon bits of your body from government buildings."

"Upset, are they?"

"Quite. Fortunately, you're being released tomorrow."

"Am I?"

"Yes. Released and deported from the country. You'll be forbidden from returning to the United States for a period of five years."

"How unfortunate."

"Now, Dickie. Be nice." She nodded at his hands. "After all, they *did* let you keep your fingernails."

The following morning at 9 AM, his cell door opened and he was ordered onto his feet. The CIA guard marched him down to the processing desk, where his personal effects were returned to him and he was required to sign some documents. As he handed back the signed paperwork, the processing agent held out a sealed envelope.

"That's for you, per the Director."

"CIA?"

"Yes, sir." The agent pressed a button under her desk and the door beside Todd buzzed. "Out through that way, sir."

Todd opened the door and found himself standing on a cement path that led to a parking area. Melissa waited at the curb in a rental car.

"We're off to the airport," she said, putting the car into gear and gliding off. "Home again, home again. Jiggedy-jig."

"I received a door prize." Todd held up the envelope.

"What is it?"

"No idea," he said. Tearing open the envelope, he peered inside.

The data drive.

Todd smirked.

"So?" Melissa nudged his arm. "What's in there?"

"Take a guess."

"It's not a bar of chocolate, is it? I hope so because I'm famished."

A LOOK AT: TALON

Book One in the Talon Series by Brent Towns

The team nobody wants, but everybody fears...

When the British government approaches the Global Corporation about stemming the flow of human trafficking across the globe, Hank Jones turns to Mary Thurston to form a team right for the job. What she pieces together is a group of misfits—no longer wanted by anyone else—with talent to burn.

Led by disgraced German Intelligence officer Anja Meyer and SAS reject Jacob Hawk, the team is autonomous, utilizing the full force of the Global Corporation and its resources as they trek across different continents in pursuit of their elusive foe—a worldwide phenomenon called Medusa.

AVAILABLE NOW

ABOUT THE AUTHOR

A relative newcomer to the world of writing, Brent Towns self-published his first book, a western, in 2015. *Last Stand in Sanctuary* took him two years to write. His first hardcover book, a Black Horse Western, was published the following year.

Since then, he has written 26 western stories, including some in collaboration with British western author, Ben Bridges.

Also, he has written the novelization to the upcoming 2019 movie from One-Eyed Horse Productions, titled, *Bill Tilghman and the Outlaws*. Not bad for an Australian author, he thinks.

Brent Towns has also scripted three Commando Comics with another two to come.

He says, "The obvious next step for me was to venture into the world of men's action/adventure/thriller stories. Thus, Team Reaper was born."

A country town in Queensland, Australia, is where Brent lives with his wife and son.

In the past, he worked as a seaweed factory worker, a knife-hand in an abattoir, mowed lawns and tidied gardens, worked in caravan parks, and worked in the hire industry. And now, as well as writing books, Brent is a home tutor for his son doing distance education.

Brent's love of reading used to take over his life, now it's writing that does that; often sitting up until the small hours, bashing away at his tortured keyboard where he loses himself in the world of fiction.

www.ingramcontent.com/pod-product-compliance
Lightning Source LLC
Chambersburg PA
CBHW010727250626
47155CB00011B/3587